Book III of The Immortal Epic

IMMORTAL GENESIS

BY
KEVIN D. BLACKMON

ASCENDANT PUBLISHING
NORTH CAROLINA
2018

Published by Ascendant Publishing

ISBN-13: 978-0-9844721-4-7

Printed in the United States of America

Also by Kevin D. Blackmon

IMMORTAL
GENESIS

ACT I

2011 AD

CHAPTER I

BEGIN TO END

"You don't know how much I've missed you," I cried, holding Seraphine tightly in my bathroom floor. "It felt as if I had lost a part of my very soul and no amount of tears could fill that void. I was afraid I had lost you forever."

"I'm sorry I frightened you. I'm sorry I left," she apologized with tears breaking from her green, elvish eyes to tumble down her face. "There's something I need to tell you, but I need to get you to a hospital first."

"No. There's no time. We need to tell Kieran that Dirk stole my power," I told her while struggling to stand from the tile floor.

"Are you well enough to stand?" she asked as she helped me to my feet.

Before I could answer, a creeping sickness came over me, causing me to lose my balance.

"No. No. No," I heard Seraphine answer her own question as she eased me back to the floor. Noticing blood on the broken tiles, she carefully inspected the back of my head. "Oh, Kevin, your head's bleeding. I'm going to call for an ambulance."

While I was lying on the cool tile, she stepped into the hall where she had dropped her purse before helping me. The room was spinning, so I closed my eyes for a moment. "Kieran," I called, but my voice sounded weak, even to myself. "Kieran, I need help. Kieran!"

I was no longer a vampire, so I was sure that I couldn't speak telepathically. Even though my powers were gone, perhaps Kieran could still hear me with his.

He and Kelena suddenly appeared in the hall next to Seraphine and were shocked to see me lying in the bathroom floor. Kelena quickly pushed through her twin brother to help me. Since becoming a being comprised of light and energy, her body passed through him like a spirit.

"Kevin, are you okay?" she asked, becoming solid, so she could lift my head up from the broken tile floor.

Before I could answer, she gasped and placed a hand on my chest. "Your powers are gone! Dirk has stolen them!"

"WHAT?" Kieran asked angrily. "Dirk was here?"

"Where is he, now?" Kelena asked even though she was probing my mind for answers.

"He's going to kill Manius," I answered.

"But killing Manius will only release the phoenix fire within him, making him as powerful as us," Kieran argued.

Recalling the attack, I told him, "Dirk used some sort of magical gauntlet to strip my immortality away. He could do the same to Manius and take all of his power before killing him."

Turning to look at her brother, Kelena said, "We must stop him before it is too late."

"Then we must hurry," he answered, fearing it may already be too late.

"Hi. You must be Seraphine," Kelena said, finally acknowledging her.

Kieran turned his attention to the tall, beautiful woman standing quietly behind him in the hallway.

"Pleased to meet you," she said with a bow of her head.

"Well, hello," Kieran greeted her, taking her hand in both of his. "My sister and I have been anxious to meet you, but please forgive our hastiness."

"I'm going with you," I told him, beginning to sit up. "We have to get to the Pentagon and warn Manius."

"Whoa! Whoa!" Kieran expressed, holding a hand out to stop me. "You can't go in your condition. You need to see a doctor."

"I'll be all right."

"And Manius isn't even at the Pentagon," he continued. "He resigned. After the meeting he had with his dark enforcers, he cleared out his desk and left for the underground warehouse in the Arctic."

"Well, let's go," I said, holding onto Kelena's arm as I stood up straight.

Glancing at his sister, "I'll leave the decision to Kel," he said before teleporting away to the Arctic warehouse.

From the expression on her face, I could tell Kelena didn't feel comfortable taking me along this time, but she nodded that she would.

"Sera too?" I asked with excitement.

With a breaking laugh and a shake of her head, she gave in. "Yes, Sera can come too."

I squeezed Kelena tightly and motioned for Seraphine to hurry over. Sensing a spark of jealousy, I let go.

"Um, you may want to dress a bit warmer there, baldy," Kelena suggested. "We are going to the Arctic Circle," she reminded me.

"Oh yeah, that's right." Feeling well enough to walk without getting dizzy, I went into my room to put on a couple layers of clothing and my hoodie. Seraphine chose one of my sweaters and a leather jacket. She put on my Superman cap and pulled her hair out through the back. I don't know what it is about a pretty girl wearing a hat, but they are exponentially prettier.

Kelena laid her hands on our shoulders and teleported us to the Arctic. I felt cold before my eyes adjusted to the darkness. I immediately crossed my arms and shivered until my body grew accustomed to the drastic change in temperature.

We were standing outside the entrance to a concrete facility built into a snow-covered mountain, the same facility where Kieran found his sister's heart. A large square above the doors emitted an eerie blue glow against a dark, starry sky.

"Kieran must already be inside," I told them. "Let's hurry." I ran to the double doors, but they were locked. "Kelena, you'll have to open the door for us?"

With a thought she unlocked it and held the

doors open for us to enter. I took hold of Seraphine's hand, and the three of us ran inside. We hurried down the lit corridor to another locked door that Kelena had to open. Seraphine and I followed her left down another icy corridor.

"What is this place?" I asked as we ran down the hall past heavy steel doors.

Surprised that she knew, Seraphine answered my question. "This is the Global Seed Vault in Norway."

"Seeds?" I asked, confused as to why they were locked away here in the Arctic.

"In case of a major catastrophe, this place is stocked with the seeds of many of the world's plants," she explained.

After passing through another airlock, we reached what appeared to be a dead end.

"The Seed Vault only masks its original purpose," Kelena added.

"Which is?" both Seraphine and I asked in unison.

With a wave of her hand, Kelena opened a magical doorway into a secret segment of the warehouse.

"Manius' armies may have driven the old races to extinction," Kelena began to explain, "but their magical artifacts were not destroyed as he made them out to be. They were collected and stored here in the mountain. Only he and Dirk knew of its location."

"Until my fellow man discovered it," Manius added as we entered the warehouse.

He stood with Vistilia and Kieran next to a large wooden crate. He wore a nice business suit like he had come straight here from his office. Vistilia wore a white sweater with jeans, a fur hat, and black boots.

"Explorers set up camp here to excavate the area and study their findings, so I had to take over management of the operation," Manius added with an expression of regret.

"You killed them," I said in disbelief.

"No, of course not," he voiced in defense. "I sent them home with no memory of their findings, so I could keep this place secret. That's when I decided it was best to hide it like Byron hid his cult many years ago. This facility is known to some as the Doomsday Vault because it's a safe haven for the world's diversity of crops in case of a Doomsday scenario. It's ironic that this place not only houses the seeds to rejuvenate life, but it also houses the power to bring about the very Doomsday that the world fears."

"Don't let him scare you," Vistilia said to ease the tension as she walked over to greet us. "Well, don't you look healthy," she said, giving me a hug. "How do you feel?"

"Slow," I answered with a disappointed laugh. "My muscles feel tight, and my body feels heavy. I miss being a vampire."

"You feel warm to me," she said with a smile.

"Excuse me," Seraphine interrupted. Her hint of jealousy caused me to smile.

Turning to her, Vistilia moved in close for a hug. "Beautiful Seraphine, how wonderful it is to finally meet you in person. My name is Vistilia." Glancing at me, she told her, "You should hang on to this young man."

"I will," she vowed with a smile at me, taking

my hand in hers.

"Now we must do something about these clothes," Vistilia said of what Seraphine chose to wear from my closet. "Those just won't do," she commented, shaking her head.

"Most of those are mine," I pointed out.

"But they're not for a lady," she laughed. Tapping her chin a moment while she thought, she made a simple wave of her hand that magically changed Seraphine's entire outfit. "Now that's much cuter," she commented.

"What do you think, Kevin?" my beloved Seraphine asked, feeling beautiful.

Looking over her, I clearly liked the new clothes. She wore black boots like the ones Vistilia had on, black leggings with a black and white skirt, and a white wool coat over a black sweater. I felt the flesh of her hand change as I held it and saw that she now had on red gloves.

"You look angelic," I answered, looking into her emerald green eyes.

Taking my hand in both of hers, she thanked me. Knowing that she is always courteous and proper, especially in public, I knew she would save me a kiss for later.

"Now, that's better," Vistilia said before moving over to Kelena.

With a gleam of fire in her eyes, she warned her, "Hug me, and I'll go supernova."

"Aww, Kelena, don't be like that," Vistilia said disappointedly. "Don't allow the werewolf's fury that still lies within you influence your emotions."

"And that is the very power that I'm talking

about," Manius pointed out.

"What do you mean?" Kieran asked, suspicious of him.

"We've grown too powerful for this world, my old friend," Manius clarified, using his bare hands to break open the lid of the crate. "Years ago, our conflicts could be contained, but now, we risk destroying everything. We are unworthy of this power."

"Why have you really come here?" Kieran questioned, lifting him with an invisible force.

"After all this time, I finally know its purpose," Manius uttered within Kieran's telekinetic grip. "We've only been caretakers. It must be contained within a single vessel. The phoenix fire isn't meant for us."

"Who? Who is it meant for?" Kieran demanded.

Before Manius could answer, Dirk teleported into the room behind me! "Well. Well. How convenient you're all here," he announced devilishly. "Thank you, Kevin, for telling everyone I was coming. You continue to prove yourself useful," he said, rubbing my bald head as he walked past me.

Kelena immediately drew her arm back, summoning a black whip that looked like a tear in space. "DO NOT TOUCH HIM!" she roared, rising into the air.

Extending the dark gauntlet that he still wore, Dirk caught the whip that snapped at him and pulled her into the gem set in the palm. She was gone! Kelena's entire body was absorbed into the blue gem!

"NO!" Kieran leaped at Dirk and transformed into a fiery tornado, engulfing him. "I will tear you apart and reabsorb you! I should have never released you!"

With the heat growing quickly in the icy room

and black lightning striking all around us, Seraphine pulled me behind a rack of large, grey plastic containers. Vistilia watched the exhilarating events unfold while Manius broke the boards of the crate he had begun opening, revealing a chiseled, black box within.

Dirk tumbled within the tornado of fire. The thick permafrost that covered everything in the room began melting and pooling up in the floor. Like his twin sister, Kieran was absorbed into the gauntlet!

Just when Manius was about to open the black box, Dirk rushed over and backhanded him across the room. Instead of killing him, he plunged his gauntlet into Vistilia's stomach! She gasped and a look of shock befell her. He pulled his hand out, and she fell to her knees. The gauntlet was covered in a strange, translucent blood. Dirk gripped the top of her head with the gauntlet, and a blue light began emanating from it.

"VISTILIA! NO! This is not the way it's supposed to happen!" Manius yelled. Leaping across the large warehouse to rescue her, Dirk caught Manius in air with an invisible force.

"No. No, father," Dirk said calmly. "Not until I finish taking mother's power. Not until I become God."

Being mortal again, I felt helpless hiding, but there was nothing I could do.

Seraphine pointed to the label on one of the containers that we were behind. It said that it contained two obsidian swords. Seraphine and I quickly pulled the container down and opened it, revealing the swords. They were crafted from metal and chiseled volcanic glass. One of the swords had a black obsidian blade and the other was green. She took the black one, so I took the other. It was surprisingly light.

Before rushing out to face what could be our deaths, Seraphine pulled my face around and kissed me. "I love you," she whispered.

"I love you, too."

The two of us ran out from behind the rack of containers. Seraphine ran behind another rack while I charged at Dirk. I raised my sword to cut away Dirk's magical gauntlet, but while he still drained knowledge from Vistilia and held Manius, a simple gaze held me in place.

Laughing, he said, "You are powerless, Kevin. What do you think you can possibly do to someone such as me?"

With my sword still above my head, I answered, "Distract you."

Just then, Seraphine leaped out from hiding and impaled him with the black obsidian sword, causing him to yell out in agony and lose his concentration.

No longer held by his paralyzing gaze, I followed through with my swing. The sword passed through his arm with no resistance from flesh or bone. It felt as though I had sliced through liquid. His arm remained intact, but the dark gauntlet fell to the floor.

Vistilia collapsed as Dirk looked down at the black blade protruding out his chest. His skin began to boil and bubble. Hot plasma burst from his skin like tiny solar flares.

"This power has corrupted you," Manius said to him.

"You're one to talk!" Dirk spat before falling to his knees. "That woman started all this! She brought suffering and death upon us all, and you still stood by her!"

"I know," Manius agreed sadly. "I'm sorry, old friend."

Lifting the lid of the black chest, Dirk was painfully ripped apart and pulled within, leaving the black sword on the floor.

Manius hurried to check on Vistilia who was still lying unconscious on the wet floor. Thick, clear blood oozed from her stomach where Dirk had punched her.

"Vistilia, can you hear me? Please be okay," he prayed, kissing her forehead and placing his cheek against hers.

The strange blood that covered her stomach seeped back into the terrible wound before healing shut. Even her white sweater repaired itself. A smile formed on her lips. "My heroes," she whispered before opening her eyes.

Breaking into a laugh, he said, "Still playing games, I see. You had me fooled with the blood."

"It's all part of the show," she explained, pulling him close for a kiss.

While Manius helped her up, Seraphine repeated, questioningly, "Part of the show? So you weren't really hurt?"

Vistilia walked over and hugged her. "I'm perfectly fine, dear. Thank you. Where I'm from, people don't live one life; we live many. We play roles in grand adventures in worlds we create."

"Will you bring my friends back to life? Bring Kieran and Kelena back," I cried.

"Be patient, sweetie. We're waiting for one more to arrive," she said, looking up at water dripping from the concrete ceiling.

"Who?" I asked.

"AMBROS!" an unfamiliar voice rang out within the large warehouse, and a figure in black silk clothing appeared sitting on the black chest. His facial features were definitely elvish; he had almond shaped eyes, thin lips, and pointy ears, but his skin wasn't like Kieran and Kelena's. His skin was the color of ash. He was a Dark Elf.

Knocking on the chest he was sitting on, he said, "It seems I've arrived just in time." Standing a slim five and half feet tall, he walked over to us.

"May I present to you, Ambros of Ashwood," Vistilia announced, and the elf bowed his head.

A Woodland Elf wearing a black silk dress appeared nearby, and Vistilia introduced her. "And Sylvia of Magestice."

Stepping toward her with open arms, Ambros said, "My dear Vistilia, haven't you grown tired yet of this game?"

With a laugh and a hug, she said, "I'm proud of you, Ambros. You've figured it out. But to answer your question, I'm actually thinking of becoming more involved."

"Don't you think you should be a bit easier on them?" he asked. "They live such short, painful lives."

"There's still much for you to learn," she said, patting him on the shoulder. She then turned to the Woodland Elf who accompanied him. "Sylvia, darling, how have you been?" she asked, hugging her lightly.

"Very well, thank you. It feels good to be home," she said with a beaming smile.

"Oh, I bet it does," Vistilia agreed. "You've had quite a trip."

"Yes, we have. We traveled to many neighboring worlds and have learned so much."

Ambros released a sudden gasp of amazement. "My swords," he said, lifting them from the water. Finally noticing the water we all were standing in from the melted permafrost, Ambros lifted his foot and shook water from it. "Let's get this mess cleaned up, shall we?" With a wave of his hand, the water gathered to the middle of the warehouse floor, and rose up to freeze in the shape of an apple tree.

In awe of the creation, Seraphine and I reached up and felt of the cold, glass-like fruit. "It's beautiful," she commented aloud.

I picked up the gauntlet from the floor to examine it. Kieran and Kelena were somehow pulled within the glowing blue gem set into the palm.

"Pop's old gauntlet," Ambros said. "I had almost forgotten about it."

"What did he use it for?" Seraphine asked him.

"He made it to absorb the life force of the Earth from the magma that often bubbled its way to the surface in Ashwood. It drained heat so that magma would quickly cool, keeping holes from erupting and destroying the city."

"Is there a way to release the energy?" I asked. "It was used on me and my friends."

Noticeably shocked, Ambros asked that I repeat what I just told him. "It was used on you?"

Nodding, I held the magical gauntlet out for him to take. He extended his hand, and the gauntlet flew to it, slipping into place. Opening and closing his fingers, Ambros looked into the blue gem.

"The power taken from you has already been

spent," Ambros explained.

"What about my friends?"

"They'll be quite all right," he assured me. "You'll see them again, soon enough." Returning to the black chest to sit down, he smiled at Manius and said, "I'd like to tell you a little tale first."

ACT II

2171 BC

CHAPTER II

THE ELVES OF LYLANDRIA

"Ambros," a sweet voice whispered to me. "Ambros," the voice called louder. I reached over, but she wasn't lying next to me. "Ambros," I heard even louder as my bed shook.

"I'm awake," I finally answered, my voice sounding thick and gravely. Rubbing my eyes, my vision began adjusting to the darkness that surrounded me and the tiny beams of light that penetrated the enveloping cocoon of plants where I slept.

"You missed the sunrise again," she told me from outside.

"I'm sorry," I apologized with a yawn. "You know I'm not a morning person. What day is it?"

"Today is . . . beautiful," she answered.

Her happiness brought a tired laugh from me. "Give me a moment, and I'll be out."

"All right but hurry up," she answered.

I clothed myself in a magical material similar to silk using a spell I had learned soon after arriving. Unlike my people, the Light Elves took nothing from animals, so the skins I wore when I arrived were burned and the ashes buried.

The vines that surrounded me divided, and I climbed out of bed to a bright, sunny day in the magnificent city of Lylandria. The fresh morning breeze carried the sweet smell of the countless flowers and fruit trees that filled the city.

"Good morning, Ambros," my mate greeted me with a kiss. Standing a couple inches taller than me, she wore a simple white and gold dress.

"Mmm, and a delightful morning to you, Jinxie," I responded.

Our home was a platform built in a large oak tree. Vines that grew at the base of the tree spiraled up to create a staircase to the platform. Vines also formed the bed where she and I slept. The others of Lylandria lived in borrows scattered throughout the city.

"I know you don't care to hear him preach, but if we hurry, we may get to the grove in time for some of today's lesson," Jinxie told me.

"Should I bring soap to this brainwashing, or will soap be provided?"

"You don't have to pay attention, just sit with me."

Agreeing to go with her, she took hold of my hand and led me down the narrow staircase to the mossy ground where we ran barefoot along paths surrounded by dew-covered flowers. Butterflies and fairies scattered to avoid us. The fairies here were similar to the

Dark Fairies of Ashwood, only they had fairer skin and brightly colored wings.

As one would imagine, the difference between Dark Elves and Light Elves was like comparing night and day. Where I had greyish skin, white hair, and sickly looking, yellow eyes, Jinxie had light skin, hair the color of orange daylilies, and bright green eyes. My people directed their magical abilities toward the dark arts of war and death where the Light Elves focused on life, beauty, and understanding the world around them. They could quickly change their hair and eye color. They also, on average, grew taller than Dark Elves.

We ran to a grove of fruit trees where many elves were gathered in a beam of sunlight discussing life.

Disappointedly, Jinxie said, "It looks like we've missed him."

I snapped my fingers sarcastically, glad that I wouldn't have to listen to the city guardian.

Jinxie picked an apple to eat.

"I believe I'll have a pear this morning," I told her as I walked over to the next tree.

The Light Elves could grow any plant they desired here in Lylandria. Through the use of magic, they kept it warmer than the surrounding region. And through magic, every plant bloomed all year long.

"There's Ambros," I heard one of the young elves say. I took a bite of my pear and sat on the moss-covered ground near the group. Jinxie sat next to me with her apple.

"So, what are we discussing today?" I asked the two dozen elves that were there.

"Why are we here," Elyon answered. He was the oldest elf present other than me. He had long, fiery red hair tied back into a ponytail.

"I don't know. You all were here before I was even awake," I answered, thinking he was asking me, not answering my question.

"No. I mean, that's what we are discussing," he clarified. "We are discussing why we are alive."

"And why are we alive?" I asked.

"The universe perceives itself through us," the violet-haired elf named Aashna explained. "We do not just live within it; we are the central part of it, and the dragons protect us because we are so special."

"Interesting view, but I don't think it's quite accurate," I said of their theory. "I mean, you could be right, but how much of the universe have you actually seen?" I asked without receiving an answer. "How much have you seen outside of this paradise?"

There was a long silence before Elyon asked, "What is the world like outside Lylandria?"

With everyone's attention on me, I answered, "Well, it's cold, harsh, and dangerous. It's not a place you should be out traveling by yourself."

"Tell us the story of when you faced the trolls," an elf boy requested.

Taking a bite of my pear, I began, "A few months ago…"

"Years," Jinxie corrected me with a laugh while chewing a bite of apple. "You're terrible at keeping up with time."

"Months make years," I defended my wordage with a smile.

"Yeah, many, many months. You've been here one hundred and fifty years."

Surprised, I asked, "Has it been that long

already?"

"Yes. I told you, you're terrible with time."

"What about the trolls?" several of the boys interrupted, anxious to hear the story that I had told many times before.

"Well, there we were," I continued, thinking back a century and a half. "Goat and I had already been traveling for weeks when we began crossing rugged mountain terrain. As we climbed down sharp cliffs, Rock Trolls ambushed us from the mountain crevasses! Standing eight feet tall," I described them, standing up and hunching my shoulders. "They were hulking beasts with thick, grey hides that blended perfectly with the mountain." I reached down and scooped up a clump of moss to sit on my shoulder. "Even moss and weeds grew on them, helping their camouflage."

Looking around, I saw that everyone was completely engrossed in my story.

"What happened next?" one of them asked.

"Very few know this about trolls because very few survive an encounter with one, but trolls love snacking on goats."

Gasps came from my listeners.

"Goat was quickly snatched up by one of the trolls and others rushed to fight over him. They ripped him apart before realizing he was only a rotten corpse. By this time, I had climbed farther down the mountain and out of their sight. I hated to leave my pet behind, but I was much too little to fight back. I, too, would have perished if I had not fled while Goat had them preoccupied. He had been carrying most of my supplies, so I lost everything that he carried. Days later, I finally reached Lylandria's warm borders with only the animal skins I wore and the two swords on my back."

"Where are they, now?" Elyon asked.

"Trolls don't live as long as elves," I answered. "I assume they died years ago."

"No. Where are your swords?"

"Oh, I keep Scourge and Devour under my bed."

"Why did you name your swords?" several elves questioned in unison.

"I didn't name them; my father did."

"Why didn't he come to Lylandria with you?"

Staring off for a moment, remembering his body being carried out of Ashwood rolled in a quilt, I answered, "He told me his journey lies along a different path," and I left it at that.

"How did you bring Goat back to life?" I was asked by a green-haired elf that we called Banks. "How do you recover a spirit from the Sun and give it flesh?"

"I haven't found a way to reunite the body with its spirit," I answered. "But there are many ways to raise the dead. With Goat, I woke him with a command directed to a specific region deep within his decomposing brain. I've also brought a hare back to life with lightning, but I wouldn't advise doing that," I told them with a laugh.

"Why not?" they all asked together.

"A bolt of lightning is a bit much for such a small creature," I began to explain. "And can a hare still be called a hare with no legs and no hair?"

Everyone laughed.

I took Jinxie's hand to help her stand. My audience clapped and thanked me for the entertaining story. I bowed to them graciously before leaving.

Jinxie and I ran hand in hand through the city to

pick a handful of strawberries. She then led me away from the others to a cave within a large growth of honeysuckle vines created by elf children. Inside the light was dim and the air had a more earthy smell than what I had grown accustomed to outside.

Jinxie looked up at how the sunlight pierced the thick canopy of honeysuckle that surrounded us. "Does this place remind you of Ashwood?"

My thoughts quickly went back to when I last spoke with my pop. He said for me to leave Ashwood and spend time with the Light Elves. He packed what few essentials I needed, and after his passing, I headed northwest to Lylandria with Goat, my undead animal companion.

"What do you remember of your childhood?" Jinxie asked.

"Before coming here, I really had only one friend," I answered sadly.

We sat down on the cool dirt. It had been cleared of leaves and packed down from kids playing there.

"Was this friend a girl or a boy?" she asked curiously.

"A young girl," I answered. "A human girl."

"A human?" she repeated. "I've never seen a human. What are they like? Are they beautiful?"

Thinking a moment how to describe them, I answered, "They are plain but friendlier than Dark Elves."

"What was her name?"

"Eve."

"That's a beautiful name. Where is she, now? Does she live in Ashwood?"

Hesitantly, I answered with a blank expression,

"She's dead."

She quickly covered her mouth. "Oh, I'm so sorry," she apologized.

"She had already cheated death once," I told her, breaking a sprout of new growth from a vine and picking the tiny leaves off one by one. "I knew when she hugged me goodbye, it would be the last time I would see her."

"You could see it," she said sadly, referring to the dark, illusory visions I have of people's skin peeling away.

Looking her in the eyes, I nodded.

"And you see me this way?" she hesitantly asked.

Turning my gaze back to the twig I held between my fingers, I nodded again. "With such a deep understanding of Necromancy, I often see the living in various states of decay, which I have no control over. Even your people, who strive for personal perfection, often appear dead to me."

"Everyone dies," she stated. "That's just something we all must accept."

I stood and took a few steps away from her. "I can't believe the Light Elves, of all creatures, would accept death without question," I told her, turning to face her.

"But there's nothing we can do to stop that," she tried to explain, walking over to me.

Pointing out to the city, I argued, "That's what he wants us to think!"

"That's what who wants us to think?"

"Kronyx, our so called 'city guardian.'"

"The dragon guardians protect us from the

outside world, so we can live a long, peaceful life," Jinxie disputed.

"Pop didn't trust them, I don't trust them, and neither should you," I pointed.

With a mocking laugh, she said, "You're just being paranoid. They protect us from trolls like the ones you faced on your way here."

"Why do you think your people all live here in this one city instead of being allowed to expand? Is it protection or imprisonment?" While her brain worked toward the question's inevitable answer, I moved on. "Whether you believe the dragons are plotting against us or not, if I can reanimate the dead, there must be a way to keep the spirit here instead of going to the Sun," I explained to her. "My friend Eve was a vampire. She could not die of disease or old age. She would have stayed young forever had she not been killed."

"So you want to become one of these vampires?"

"No. I don't, but like raising the dead, there must be many ways one can become immortal."

"The Sun is our true home. We all must make that journey after the body dies," she preached, reciting her words exactly as they had been preached to her.

"Don't be so narrow minded. Not only could we live in this paradise forever, we could spread it over the entire world. We could bring back everyone who has passed on!"

"Death Magic is prohibited here. You know this."

"If I could save people from death, wouldn't that then be considered Life Magic? How would that be any different from what you do already with these plants?"

I questioned.

"The plants we grow still live and die just like everything else. We use magic only to keep them fruitful and productive throughout their lifetime," she explained.

"Well, what if we had a choice to live another lifetime or more?" I asked to soften my apparently radical vision. "What if you and I could wake up to a countless number of sunrises? What if we could spend many, many lifetimes enjoying this paradise your people have created?"

Smiling, she answered, "That does sound nice, but you'll have to wake up for those sunrises to enjoy them with me."

We both laughed, and I took hold of her hand, leading her to me. The honeysuckle that surrounded us barely allowed us to stand without having to stoop. Marveling at her big, beautiful eyes, I pressed my lips delicately to her nose before moving to her lips.

"You kiss with your eyes shut," she noted, giggling sweetly. "Are you afraid you'll have one of your dead visions of me?"

"It's not funny," I told her, unable to hold back my laughter. "I may like controlling the dead, but I don't like kissing them."

With an intrigued look on her face, she whispered, "You've been experimenting in secret, haven't you? Kronyx will ban you for bringing Death Magic to Lylandria. You agreed not to use it when you arrived."

"Necromancy may be banned within Lylandria, but there are no rules about practicing it beyond the city borders," I answered with a sly grin. "You didn't think

I'd quit for all these months I've been here, did you?"

She slapped me lightly across the chest. "Years!" she corrected me again, laughing as she chased me out of the honeysuckle cave.

I ran through the city to some raspberry bushes where I began picking them to throw at her. She screamed and took cover behind another bush. I stood up to throw a berry just in time to see her throw one at me. Instead of ducking, I opened my mouth to eat it only for it to bounce off my cheek. We both laughed and continued throwing raspberries at each other, drawing the attention of many others. Elves and fairies of all ages soon began gathering raspberries and other small fruits, and for most of the afternoon, the entire city was at war!

Growing tired of battle, Jinxie and I slipped away to wash fruit juice from our face and arms. A simple spell removed the stains from our clothing.

"Would you like to come with me to check my traps?" I asked Jinxie while she sat in the grass, brushing her radiant orange hair.

"Traps? What kind of traps?"

"I trap small animals to study," I answered. "I check them every few days."

"Okay," she nervously agreed.

I took her hand to help her stand and led her to the tall hedges that surrounded Lylandria. I pulled back the limbs to allow Jinxie to slip through the hidden, narrow passage that I had secretly trimmed through the green wall. I followed, releasing the limbs to close the way behind us. We stepped out from the hedges into a snow-covered land. Bare trees dotted white, rolling hills, and a light snow blew on the wind.

Jinxie gasped at the sight. "It's frozen! Is this

where you've been coming when you say you're going for an evening walk?"

"It is. What do you think?" I asked proudly, taking a deep breath of the bitter air while I magically added a thicker layer of clothing.

"It's cold," she answered with a shiver. "Why is it so bleak and dreadful?"

"This is the real world. Out here, the world cycles through warm and cold seasons. Lylandria would look like this if it wasn't augmented by magic."

Seeing that I had already added clothing, she did the same before I led her to one of my animal traps not far away.

"This is it," I said, bending down next to a hole dug in the ground. "Oh, this is a good catch!"

Jinxie looked over curiously while I reached into the heap of snow that nearly filled the hole. "What is it?"

Feeling over the cold body, I located a leg to take hold of and pulled the stiff carcass from the snow.

Stepping back, Jinxie was preparing herself to be disgusted. "What is that?"

"It's a fox," I answered, placing it on the ground next to us and reaching back into the hole for a second animal.

Surprised, she asked, "There's another?"

I laughed a little and laid a partially eaten, frozen rabbit next to the fox. "Yeah, how 'bout that? I caught two animals in one trap."

"The hole isn't very deep. Why couldn't they have just jumped out?" she asked curiously.

"After digging the hole," I began to explain, scooping out the snow, "I placed a bit of food in to lure a rabbit." I then pushed snow away from the edges and began tracing a line in the dirt around the hole. "I cast a spell over the hole allowing things to enter but not escape. The fox tried to take my catch, but he, too, was caught before the spell wore off."

"Now that you have them, what do you plan to do with them?"

Closing my eyes, I took a deep breath and carefully placed my hands on both animals. "I can bring their bodies back to life," I whispered as they began to twitch. "I can see glimpses of their memories," I continued, struggling to understand. "But I still can't recombine the two." I opened my eyes and pulled my hands away from the dead animals, sighing in frustration.

"What's holding you back?" Jinxie asked softly.

I rubbed my head, giving her question serious thought. "Whether it's been months or minutes, dead is dead."

She placed a hand on mine. "You'll figure it out. You just need time."

"Time," I repeated. "Time will run out for us all, if I don't."

"Then I'll help you."

Surprised, I asked, "But what if we're both banned from Lylandria?"

"Then we'll be banned together," she answered sweetly, kissing me on the nose.

"We have a lot of work to do," I told her with a smile. "We'll get started after dark."

I stood to leave, but Jinxie stopped me. "Wait! We must help these animals return to the earth."

She placed her hands over the animals, but

instead of trying to bring them to life as I did, the animals caught fire and quickly collapsed into small piles of ash that she covered with snow. We then followed our tracks back to my secret passage into Lylandria and headed home.

As the last rays of sunlight receded, giving way to starlight, Jinxie and I watched the clouds roll by while lying back on a carpet of moss. Jinxie held her hand out for me to take in mine. I gladly took it.

Turning my head to look at her, I asked, "How did I end up with the most perfect woman in existence?"

Looking into my yellow eyes, she answered, "Because you are you, and I am me. We're only perfect together. I love you more than anything in the universe."

Glancing up at the night sky, I commented, "From here, it appears there's not all that much out in space."

Surprised by the remark, she rolled over on me and began tickling me. "Ambros, you're so mean!"

I couldn't speak from laughing while futilely protecting sensitive areas. She poked, prodded, and gouged until I could no longer breathe!

"Had enough? Had enough?"

I shook my head no, so she continued tickling me a bit longer. She then took my face in her hands and kissed me. "The universe of the mind is limitless and full of wonders beyond reckoning."

"Oh, I'm sorry," a small voice said over us.

Looking up, we saw a fairy with her back to us. Her blonde, braided ponytail reached all the way to her feet.

"It's all right, Alana," Jinxie told her. "What is it that you need?"

Without turning around to look at us, she said, "Kronyx requests to see Ambros."

I thanked her for relaying the message, and she flew off into the darkness. "I wonder what he needs to see me about," I thought aloud.

"Well, he just returned from a meeting with the World Council," Jinxie mentioned while still sitting on me. "He may have news concerning Ashwood."

Propping up on my elbows, I told her, "That's what I'm afraid of."

She kissed my nose before getting off of me and helping me stand.

I ran my fingers behind her neck and through her soft, orange hair. I suddenly saw the flesh of her face dissolve away, revealing the muscles beneath, and I closed my eyes.

"Ambros," she called. "Ambros, you're having one of your visions, aren't you?"

I nodded, and she held me close. "I'm sorry," I whispered.

"It's okay. I'm right here, and I'm perfectly healthy."

Embarrassed by my problem, I pulled away from her. "I suppose I should head on to see what Kronyx wants to see me about."

"All right, but if you're not back soon," she shook her finger, "I'll come save you from the mean ol' dragon," she teased, pulling me close for another kiss.

"I'll be watching for you," I pointed at her before walking through the dimly lit garden to meet with the city guardian in his dwelling.

After sunset, the elves of Lylandria hung fairy fire lanterns at the entrance to their homes. It was a tradition that symbolized life and how it will pass through darkness to see the sun again.

I walked down the stone steps that led deep into Kronyx's borrow. The staircase opened into a large room with walls constructed of thick glass. It was illuminated by large, white crystals positioned around the room on glass pedestals. Even tables and shelves were made of glass. The floor, though, wasn't dirt like in most dwellings but a thick carpet of moss. With eyes shut and legs crossed as if sitting on an invisible chair, Kronyx floated within the center of the ring of crystals meditating.

Kronyx was a Yellow Dragon but took the form of an elder Light Elf. He had long, silky blond hair that drifted like smoke around his head, and he wore a white robe with gold accents that ran like a vine through the material.

"You called for me?" I asked, but he did not respond. "Kronyx?"

"The humans believe they are the center of the universe, that their lives have meaning," he finally spoke while remaining in a meditative state. "They believe godly, humanlike beings are concerned with their day to day struggles, but they lack the ability to see the bigger picture. Their lives do have meaning, but not in the way they believe. My time with the Light Elves has shown me that they are not so different. Like the humans, they fill in areas of the unknown, namely the period of time after the body dies, with how they envision an everlasting perfect day with their ancestors in the Sun."

"And what do you see?" I asked, interrupting his monologue while rubbing a hand over one of the glowing crystals' facets.

"I see infinity in all directions."

The room suddenly went dark, and I pulled my hand away from the crystal thinking I had done something I shouldn't. Twinkling starlight began to show on the walls as if we were viewing the night sky. I stepped closer to the center of the room and looked up in awe as the cosmos whirled overhead, a maelstrom of beautiful chaos and simplistic order. I saw the very heat from stars stripped away by invisible forces while others lit unknown worlds. Debris coalesced in the darkness to form new planets and join their brothers in a long dance around their sun.

"I see the birth and death of stars, their scattered remains repurposed by the universe. What seem like random occurrences are actually unseen forces at work, for the universe is God. Or to be more precise, will be God. As life emerges and spreads throughout the universe, God becomes more and more aware of himself."

The stars around us faded, and the white crystals once again lit the room. Kronyx slowly lowered to a pillow that was on the mossy floor below him, and his closed lids suddenly opened to reveal the gold, reptilian eyes within. "Don't you see, Ambros? God is made of us."

Standing before him, I asked, "Has life spread throughout the entire universe?"

"No, but this planet has been visited by life from other worlds."

"How do you know this?"

"I met with the World Council and spoke with the new guardian of Ashwood…"

"Wait a moment," I interrupted. "The new

guardian? What happened to Magnus?"

"Magnus," he hissed. "The traitor murdered the heads of the council and was cast into the Abyss of the Dead."

I laughed, "Sounds like a holiday." I turned to walk away.

"You jest?"

"You'll have to excuse my dark sense of humor."

Kronyx placed his feet on the soft mossy floor. "You were named after Ambrosius the Yellow, were you not?"

"Yes," I answered, watching a worm push its way through the rich earth on the opposite side of the glass wall.

"He raised you, did he not? Do you still miss him?" he asked probing futilely for a glimpse of my memories.

I nodded, seeing Kronyx's reflection in the glass. "Of course, I miss him. He was the only family I ever knew. He was like a father to me." I worded my answer carefully.

"Did he ever tell you the story of the great Dragon King Shadowrath?"

"It was one of many bedtime stories he told me," I answered, turning to face him. "Shadowrath died in combat with a powerful creature called a phoenix, didn't he?"

"Yes. Arethil was the creature's name," he said, walking over to pull a scroll from the shelf. "I've been working for centuries piecing the legend together. When Lylandria was in need of a new guardian, I felt it would be a great opportunity to hear the old tale from the Light

Elves' perspective."

"What did you learn?"

"Arethil was described as taking many forms. Her most common form was of a bird but unlike any bird from this world," he said with a bit of excitement. I walked over to the table where he unrolled a painting of a brightly colored bird with big eyes and a beautiful woman with very long, strawberry blonde hair.

Pointing to the woman, I asked, "Who's that?"

"This is the other form she took. Stories told that she could augment her size and become intangible at will, pass through solid objects, and travel great distances in an instant."

"This is very interesting, Kronyx, but what does all this have to do with me?"

"I would like you to help me fill in the gaps of this story."

"I don't know what you're talking about."

"No, I believe you do," Kronyx said circling around me. "I believe you were there."

"Excuse me?"

"I have reason to believe you are Ambrosius reincarnated."

"That's ridiculous," I laughed, remembering Pop's work on regeneration and the materials he used to create me. I could not reveal how I was given life to this serpent. "I believe that it's time for me to be heading home."

I turned to leave, but vines quickly sprouted from the mossy floor to restrain me. "Is all this really necessary?" I asked, glancing down at the vines.

He stepped close to me. "You will answer my questions," he said in a stern tone.

"Have you asked a question?" I joked.

"Are you Ambrosius reincarnate?" he yelled in my face.

My eyes squinted and my head turned away from his hot breath. "I wish I were Ambrosius; I would burn your ass where you stand," I cursed with a laugh, my patience wearing thin.

"HAHAHA! I anticipated you wouldn't give information to me freely. I am well aware of your distrust of my kind."

I twitched, feeling Kronyx probing my mind again. "You won't find anything in there but cobwebs and dead things," I uttered.

"You must have a powerful mind, Dark Elf, to keep one such as me from hearing your thoughts," he declared, circling around me. "But no matter; these crystals not only enhance my vision into the cosmos, but they also enhance my telepathic abilities to see into the mind. I'll learn all of yours and Ambrosius' secrets soon enough."

The vines began pulling me to the center of the room where Kronyx had been meditating. I was still standing upright, but my feet were not touching the mossy floor.

"The guardian of Ashwood is looking for you," he said to me as I was positioned within the center of the ring of crystals, "and I would like to know why."

Kronyx sat on the floor in front of me. Once again, I felt him reach into my mind. He began floating, rising to become eye level. Light within the crystals dimmed, and I felt bolts of energy sparking along my scalp. He slapped me on the side of the head, and a vision of him slapping me appeared on the walls around us. His head jostled, too, at the moment of impact. "That's better," he said aloud. "We're now connected."

He was quiet for a moment, taking long, deep breaths. And then he began to speak. "Centuries ago, my father created a looking glass that allowed him to peer deep into space. He realized that he wasn't just looking at distant worlds but actually looking through time itself. I continued his work to find that I could use living creatures to see a sort of lineage deep into the past."

The walls depicted scenes from my memories. I had no control over what he could see. I saw myself holding Jinxie within our enclosed bed of vines. I saw my journey to Lylandria with Goat. I saw Eve hug me goodbye outside my home in Ashwood.

"I told you the truth, Kronyx. I am not Ambrosius."

"Oh, I believe you, young elf, but I intend to look beyond you," he divulged. "By using you as a focal point, my enhanced telepathic ability will allow me to see deep into the past."

Around me, I saw Magnus bite Ambrosius. I tried closing my eyes but could still see him drained of blood. I then saw Pop creating another like me only to pass to them his consciousness during meditation. I saw him do this over and over."

"Ah, I see Ambrosius did in fact live for millennia by growing himself new bodies, but for some reason, he chose not to use you as he did the others."

I saw elves mining a cave. They chipped a wall of stone that broke away to a shaft into a volcano. A fair-skinned Ambrosius used a magical gauntlet to absorb the heat from the lake of magma below to create solid stone.

"Within the fabric of time," he began to explain, "lies a record of every creature that has lived, every deed that has been done, and every word that has been spoken. Reaching that information is exceptionally difficult, unless you have a physical link connecting the present to the past."

"Are you also capable of seeing the future?"

"The ocean of time is immeasurably vast, and the currents leading into the future are treacherous and too unpredictable to produce a clear, singular vision."

The walls showed Pop casting a powerful spell on a black obsidian chest that entrapped the charred remains of a dragon and a large, colorful bird. The chest was cast into the Abyss of the Dead.

"So that is why she needs you," Kronyx presumed, thinking aloud. "Since Ambrosius locked Shadowrath and Arethil within the chest, she believes you can release them. Then she must also believe you can resurrect them."

"But I..."

He opened his reptilian eyes, the vertical pupils narrowing to focus on me. "Don't think I sit idly down here with my eyes shut to all beyond these glass walls. I know of your late night walks to the city's border," he revealed. "I've seen you butcher woodland animals only to call them back from the dead."

I remained quite as he began pacing the floor.

"But which of the legendary creatures does she plan to resurrect, I'm not entirely sure." He continued, his mind working to piece together what he knew and what he believed to be true. "She must have the chest!" he finally blurted out.

"Perhaps she just wants to know how I'm doing," I mentioned sarcastically.

Kronyx laughed. "Yndra doesn't care about your well-being. She wants what we all want—power. She has control over Ashwood and no doubt has her sights set on taking head position of the World Council. Just like Elsbareth, her vision is far too narrow. They set their greedy eyes on ruling the Earth but…"

"AH HA!" I burst. "I knew it!"

"Did you really need confirmation?" he asked with a grin. "Convincing you that we are not evil is just as difficult as convincing the rest of your race that we are."

"But you are evil."

"Evil is a point of view. I'm doing this for your own good," he argued calmly.

"And what is it you plan to do with the information you've gotten from me?"

Vines quickly whipped around my face, covering my mouth to keep me quiet, and I found myself slowly being pulled into the ground!

"Whatever her plan may be, we cannot allow Yndra to get her conniving claws on you now, can we?" he asked, but I could only mumble while I struggled against the vines that held me. "I will protect you and the rest of the world by burying you."

Behind him, I saw Jinxie come down the stairs. She saw that I was in trouble and looked afraid for me.

"Ah, Jinxie, I'm so glad you could join us." Kronyx said before turning to face her.

The tip of a black sword suddenly protruded from his back! Jinxie had brought my swords with her, fearing I may truly be in danger. She pulled the sword from his chest, but he released his fiery breath, incinerating her instantly!

I screamed behind my mask of vines as I fought to break free.

Kronyx fell to his knees. The wound I saw on his back burned with the black fire from Devour as it spread throughout his body, crystallizing organs and turning blood into ash. His fingers dug into the mossy floor to pull himself around to no doubt burn me, too. His mouth opened but only his dying breath came forth.

The power he held over the vines released its grip, and I was able to pull myself free. I leaped over Kronyx's body as it began reverting to its original form. There was nothing left of my beloved Jinxie. She had been reduced to ash.

"Argh, this makes bringing you back difficult."

I folded the hem of my tunic over to make a pocket. The material magically fused, and I pulled it away to create a pouch. I pushed some of Jinxie's hot ashes into the pouch, and pinched the opening shut. I then pulled a string from thin air and tied the bag of ashes to my belt.

Kronyx had taken the form of an elf, but now that he was dead, his shriveling corpse was changing back into a Yellow Dragon, a very large Yellow Dragon. I heard the glass walls and furniture shattering around me as his body quickly filled his burrow. Tears fell from my eyes as I quickly grabbed up my two obsidian swords that Jinxie had taken from under our bed, and I ran for the stairs. I reached the surface just as the ground caved in behind me.

All the elves came running out of their homes to see what had happened and found me standing outside the city guardian's collapsed home.

"What happened here, Ambros? Is everyone all right? Where is Kronyx?" I was asked by many of the surrounding elves.

Glancing back at the cave in, I mumbled, "This won't turn out well."

Nazir, one of the Light Elf elders, stepped from the growing crowd to question me. Placing a hand on my shoulder, he asked, "Are you all right, son?"

"I lost Jinxie," I answered sadly.

"What about Kronyx? Is he still in there?" he asked worriedly.

"Forget Kronyx! We're all in danger!"

"What are you talking about?"

"The dragons have us in the dark about their true motives," I began. "They keep us feeling safe and happy while they secretly gain power enough to conquer us and the rest of the world!"

"Did you hit your head?" I heard someone else ask.

"The World Council assigns, who you are led to believe, a dragon guardian to each of the elf cities and to different regions of the world, but not to protect them, to make sure no one race becomes too powerful while the dragons gather an army in the east!"

"I'm going to ask you again," Nazir said in a sterner tone. "What happened here, cousin?"

Taking a deep breath, I answered, "Kronyx summoned me because the guardian of Ashwood is hunting for me. By looking into my past, he reached the conclusion that she may have found Arethil's remains, and…"

Laughter rang out around me.

"The legendary phoenix?" the elder asked. He, too, chuckled at my claims.

"He did hit his head," I heard someone from the crowd say just as I felt blood trickle down my face from the scalp of my hair.

Elyon pointed. "No, that's dragon blood!"

Gasps were heard from all around me.

"Ambros, we're going to have to ask that you hand over your swords and come with us," Nazir ordered.

"For what? Kronyx was going to kill me!"

"That's not for us to determine," the elder said calmly.

Two elves snuck up behind me and grabbed my wrists. "Drop your weapons, cousin," they demanded.

"Unhand me! I don't want any trouble!"

"We don't either," one of the elves said as he struggled to hold me.

"We must restrain you until a council representative arrives and digs up Kronyx's remains, so we can see the body for ourselves," Nazir explained.

While still held by the two elves, I began to laugh. "So you want to see Kronyx's remains? You want to see him? Let me call him for you."

With that, I sent a thought out to the dragon's dead mind. I felt his body shudder beneath the earth. Everyone held their balance and suddenly looked frightened for what was happening.

"Did Kronyx survive?" someone asked.

I laughed. "I'm unafraid not."

Behind me, the collapsed burrow of our city guardian heaved, knocking everyone down. The fearsome dragon burst out from the collapsed earth and released a bone-chilling roar! The flesh had dissolved beneath his dull and dirty yellow scales, making his thick hide sag and appear as if it were melting away.

No longer being held by the two elves, I slung my sheathed swords over my shoulder and ran toward Kronyx. The dragon bowed his head for me to climb on. I sat between the horns on his head as he took flight.

CHAPTER III

THE FALL OF THE GIANTS

Beyond Lylandria's border, the winter winds chilled me to the bone. I summoned warmer clothing and steered my zombie dragon east toward the World Council Palace. I remembered visiting the Dragon Cavern as a child with Pop, so I knew about where it was located. And with the serpent's mind I now controlled, I was sure I would have no trouble finding my way.

After well more than a century of dealing with the dead, I had developed a special connection with them. I was capable of seeing their entire life even if they were completely brainless. It was a very narrow view similar to how Kronyx used me to see into the distant past. All Pop had to do was meditate to see through time. He didn't need anything to direct his vision. Perhaps, someday, I'll be just as powerful.

"Jinxie," I exhaled as the weight of reality came back to me. My dear Jinxie was burned to ash. Even if I could reach into her past and gather her consciousness, she has no body to come back to. I wiped frozen tears from my eyes and tried to busy my mind from thoughts of her.

Even though the clouds beneath me were thin, the light of the crescent moon wasn't enough to illuminate the forest far below. Surrounded by nothing but cold darkness, I laid my head on the dragon's scales. My eyes begged for sleep, but my thoughts would not rest. The hours passed slowly while the pain swelled, but the sun finally broke over the distant mountains, and nestled among them was an immense tower.

"The dragons' claws have been busy."

I gave a mental command for Kronyx to land, so he lowered us through the morning fog to a dew-covered flower garden surrounding a marble palace. Now that he was an undead dragon, Kronyx could no longer use magic to change his form, so he plopped down on a large area of flowers, mashing them into the dirt. Lowering his head, I slid off and told him to lay quietly until I called for him.

Taking a deep breath, I needed to clear my mind of Jinxie's death, so I could focus on my next task. I took another deep breath of the fresh, morning air and skipped along a stone path that wound around groups of flowers and trees to the palace. With both fists, I knocked out a rhythm on the large double doors until someone opened them.

"A pleasant morning to you, cousin," a Wood Elf greeted me with a smile. "Welcome to the World Council Palace. My name is Tully. I will lead you to

Assam the Yellow for registration. Please, follow..."

"Snap!" I interrupted, grabbing his head and breaking his neck! I quickly dragged his body outside and took a dagger from the elf's belt to cut my finger. "I'm sorry, Tully, but I'd like to go about my business unnoticed. I could use your help, though," I told him as I dropped a bit of blood in each of his eyes and woke him from the dead.

With his mouth hanging open and his head still twisted at an unnatural angle, the elf slowly picked himself up from the ground.

"Oh, this won't do. Hold your head up and close that mouth," I commanded, adjusting his head and slapping his mouth shut.

He stared at me blankly, his mouth dropping back open.

"I guess this is as good as it's going to get. Would you be so kind to give me a tour?"

The zombie elf gave me an agreeing moan, and I followed him inside.

The World Council Palace was like nothing I had ever seen before. Through tall windows, I could see the morning sun rising over the surrounding mountains to reflect off beautiful marble walls. There was no one else besides us on the ground level of the tower, but I could see a few elves high above us on a spiraling walkway.

"I'm hungry," I said aloud after my stomach reminded me that it was time for breakfast. "Where can I get some food around here?"

The zombie made his way to a door and pushed it open. I followed him outside and across a covered walkway that led to a single story building with smoke puffing out of the chimney. I gave a command for the zombie to stay where he was while I went inside; I didn't want to draw any attention if I could help it.

It was surprisingly cool inside considering the large fire burning in the center of the room. The fire burned in a long fire pit where animals roasted on spits and stews simmered in pots. Herbs and cured meats hung from the ceiling, and preparation tables covered in various fruits and vegetables lined the walls. A dozen elves were busy cooking and preparing food.

"A glorious morning to you, dear cousin," I was greeted by one of the cooks as he pulled a pot from the fire.

"Thank you. And a glorious morning to you."

The elf dipped a small wooden spoon into the stew and handed it to me. I lifted the spoon to my nose. It smelled delicious, so I tasted it. "Mmm. This is amazing. What is it?"

The elf took a loaf of bread that had been hollowed out and filled it with the delicious stew. Handing it to me, he called it, "Griffin corn chowder."

"I've never heard of corn before." I took another bite of the hearty soup and bowed graciously before leaving.

Outside, my tour guide waited right where I had left him. I followed the dead elf across the walkway back to the palace tower while eating my stew. The zombie reached the door and pushed against it like he did before, but it did not open.

"Pull, mush brain. It's pull in, push out," I explained.

Rubbing his hand on the door, he clearly couldn't open it, so I opened it for him and followed him inside. Looking up the center of the tower, I said, "Now I need to find out what devilish tricks the dragons have up their scales."

I caught a vision from Tully's mind of a library in an upper level of the tower. "That's a start. Lead the way."

While I ate my stew and followed Tully up the spiraling walkway, I began singing an old song that I remembered elflings singing in Ashwood. "Animal clavicles in my soup. Maggots and zombies loop the loop."

The elves we met along the way noticed that their palace doorman seemed sick that morning and wished him a speedy recovery. I told them he would be fine. He just needed to sleep it off.

Tully led me to a large room with shelves holding many books. Looking over the books, I finished my soup and ate the bread bowl. I decided I should ask Tully for help. "I'm looking for something written within the past century or so that tells a bit about what the Dragon Council have been doing."

Tully shuffled over to a section and dragged his fingers weakly over the spine of a book that looked new in comparison to the others on the shelves.

"The Fall of the Giants by Assim the Yellow," I read aloud before taking it to one of the chairs. I unstrapped the swords from my back, so I could sit comfortably. I didn't have to read much into the story to find the names of Magnus and Dirk who I remembered from years past. There was also mention of a Dark Elf named Byron. Pictures drawn of the three instantly grabbed my attention. "That's Pop!" Even without the eye patch, the pictures drawn of Byron were unmistakably Ambrosius.

While I read, Tully wandered around the room aimlessly, paying no attention to the gorgeous mountain vista seen from the large windows.

The story told of Grimlash, the five heads of the World Council, ordering his council members to aid the dragon guardians in protecting the elf cities from approaching armies. The Sea Giants mobilized to attack the Light Elves of Lylandria, the Fire Giants planned an attack on the Dark Elves of Ashwood, and the Storm Giants marched against the Woodland Elves of Snowcrest.

"Rubbish!" I blurted out. "It's the same lies they've fed us for ages. Oh, we're protecting the elves," I mocked. "The dragons are only protecting us until they're ready to eat us," I added with a chomp and smack of my lips.

After defeating the giants, Magnus the Red Dragon Lord sought to kill his fellow council members and take the thrown as head of the World Council. He succeeded in killing Valik the Black Dragon Lord and Grimlash the Hydra before being defeated by Elsbareth the White Dragon Lord. For his crimes against the World Council, he was cast into the Abyss of the Dead. Elsbareth became the new head of the council and appointed the task of record keeping and electing new members to Assim. No longer needing to safeguard the northern road, the elves of Snowcrest moved south to a more temperate climate, and with the help of dragons, they began construction of a magnificent city for dragons and elves alike. They named the city Magestice.

My eyes were growing heavy. "I'm so tired," I mumbled to myself. "But I want to read all that . . . .

My eyes opened, and I stretched. I had fallen asleep while reading. The sun had already set and starlight shined through the windows to partially illuminate the library.

Standing from my chair, I stretched again. "I slept like the dead. Speaking of which.... Tully?"

I strapped my swords to my back and picked the book up I had been reading from the floor where it had fallen from my lap. I then began searching the library for the undead elf. I closed my eyes a moment to see through Tully's eyes, so perhaps I could find him. I saw elves screaming! I saw torn flesh! I saw blood!

I rushed to the library door and pushed it open to find the palace in chaos! Tully had left the library and infected others, turning them into starving zombies. Most of the elves that lived within the palace frantically ran for the exits while others tried to fight off their undead friends and loved ones.

"Well, this place sure livened up nicely," I commented to myself. While carrying the book under my arm, I casually made my way through the carnage to the ground floor. The ravenous zombies paid no mind to me but scrambled toward everyone else in sight.

I was caught up in the rush of elves as they pushed to get out, but outside, they faced another monster—my undead Yellow Dragon. Leaving Kronyx to be dealt with by the dragons, the elves made for the surrounding forests.

Beneath dim moonlight, three mighty serpents fought viciously, trampling a large area of the palace gardens. Kronyx fought a Blue and a White Dragon on the ground while others circled the dark skies above. His body was riddled with deep slashes and bites, but he had no blood to pour from them.

I needed Kronyx to fly me away from there before I was discovered as the cause of the madness, so I sent a mental command to the infected elves within the palace. Dozens came outside to attack the dragons. The zombie attacks provided just enough of a distraction for Kronyx to sink his teeth into the White Dragon's exposed neck. I then sent a command for us to escape, so he pushed past the dragons and galloped to me. He grabbed me loosely in his massive jaws and leaped into the air. The Blue Dragon sent a bolt of lightning through the zombies that attacked him, disintegrating many of them before he followed us.

Several of the dragons that were circling overhead landed to destroy what zombies remained while another Yellow Dragon joined the Blue that chased me into the night. I steered Kronyx as if controlling my own body, but I didn't know where I was heading. I knew only that I had overstayed my welcome at the Council Palace.

I flew for a long while. I reached a large body of water, but, seeing land ahead, I continued west.

Using Kronyx's keen dragon eyesight, I could see that we were still being followed. A terrible storm was called to darken the skies and hinder my vision. It became difficult to fly through the torrential rain and heavy winds, so I pushed Kronyx to climb above the storm. I kept his jaws clenched shut to keep the rain from blowing in on me while I concentrated on using his eyes to see. Thunder boomed and bolts of lightning flashed all around us.

When we finally broke through the storm clouds, I found the two dragons were waiting for me. Fire came from the Yellow Dragon's gapping maw, searing Kronyx's withered flesh and burning his leathery wings. Without them, I couldn't stay aloft, so Kronyx fell with me locked inside.

"Son of an imp!" I cursed as I braced myself for the inevitable impact that I was unsure I would walk away from.

Outside, I heard the storm raging and the wind howling with my descent. The impact came, but it wasn't solid. Salt water seeped into the mouth of Kronyx.

"I'm in the ocean!"

I ordered Kronyx to open his mouth for me to escape, and his jaws opened, letting water rush in. I glanced only briefly at him as he sank into the deep before I fought against the turbulent waters to reach the surface. I couldn't tell which direction I was from the shore while the storm surged. All I could do was try to keep my head above water until it subsided.

Hours later, I finally washed ashore, but I was so exhausted I lay on the beach long after the conjured storm dissipated. The events of the past two days began playing over and over in my head. I had lost it all. Once again, my life was gone. "Jinxie," I cried into the sand.

CHAPTER IV

CAPTAIN LORENA

When the morning tide began washing over my face, I felt it was time to get myself up. There was not a cloud in the sky and not a soul in sight. I felt for my swords and was relieved that they were still sheathed on my back. I removed them and stripped off my ruined clothes to wash the sand from my matted hair and skin. I opened the pouch that I still carried on my belt to examine the ashes within and found them to be perfectly dry. I magically wove myself a new set of clothing and continued following the coastline on foot.

I walked all day. I was tired, sore, smelly, and hungry. Along the beach, the remains of spidery crustaceans were left by birds.

As the sun set, I saw what looked to be torch light far up the beach. I pushed myself to continue on instead of stopping to rest.

The torches burned along an inlet that led into a harbor with a single ship docked. I stepped up on a creaky, wooden walkway that led to a large building with several small huts built beyond it. As I approached, I heard thumping music coming from within. A sign hanging above the door depicted the legs of one of those crustaceans I saw on the beach and the fan-shaped tail of another creature.

I opened the door to a bustling restaurant. A band played drums while women wearing next to nothing danced on and around tables of food. Everyone was drinking and praising the hostess as she made her way around to greet everyone. She wore a white shirt tied tightly to hug her womanly figure, a red dress with sandals, and a large red hat that sat at a sharp angle atop her head.

"Where did you get all that beautiful blonde hair?" a man asked the hostess, rubbing a lock of it between his fingers.

Staring him straight in the eyes, she answered, "I stole it . . . from my mother." She smacked his jaws and walked away, bringing a laugh from everyone in the restaurant.

"What about those gorgeous blue eyes?" another man flirted, pulling her to him.

"They're from drinking too much sea water," she smiled, taking his mead away and drinking it down in one gulp. Handing the mug back to him, she dropped it on his foot before he could take hold of it.

"How 'bout you untie those kittens there, kitten?" a man asked as he took hold of a string that held her shirt closed but struggled with the knot.

"How 'bout I help you with that," she offered,

unsheathing a knife. As she brought the knife up, she severed his belt. His pants fell to his ankles, and everyone burst with laughter. "Whoops," she voiced, covering her lips bashfully. While the man hurried to pull his breeches up, she effortlessly pushed him over. "And it's not kitten; it's Captain," she corrected him. Stepping up on a table, she took her hat off and bowed theatrically, bringing cheers from the people. "Captain Lorena."

I made my way over to a long table covered with all sorts of exotic food and filled a plate with as much as it would hold. I then grabbed a full mug of mead and sat down. It felt good to rest and put food in my belly. Staring at my plate, I soon forgot about the humans making merriment around me.

"Who are you?" a woman carrying a large pitcher of mead asked, startling me from my dinner.

"Uh…"

"Captain!" she called out.

The charismatic hostess walked over to my table and turned a chair around, sitting in it backwards. "I've heard tales of Dark Elves, but you're the first I've laid eyes on."

I glanced around to see that everyone was staring at me.

"Yeah, you're a scene stealer, but how were you planning to pay for all this? I'm not running a charity for outsiders here, you know."

"I was hungry, so I filled a plate."

She laughed loudly. "A fellow pirate! I like you already. You're welcome to eat and drink to your heart's content. My name is Captain Lorena, owner of Legs & Tail," she announced, waving a hand out to the restaurant which slowly began resuming its evening festivities of drinking, dining, and dancing.

"I'm Ambros of Ashwood," I told her, licking the mead from my lips.

"Mmm. Sounds like an exciting place for a girl like me."

Catching her dirty comment, I repeated more clearly, "I said Ashwood."

"I know what you said," she winked. "So how did you find this place?"

"I was caught in a storm and washed ashore not far from here."

"I know these waters. I know the surrounding lands. There are no elves here." She took a bite of food from my plate and washed it down with a swallow of my mead. "It's impolite to keep a girl waiting."

"My business is my own."

"Not when you're in my restaurant," she argued.

I felt the swords on my back being quickly unsheathed. Just as I was standing to face the person behind me, the blonde captain threw a dinner plate, striking me across the brow.

I awoke in a small, wooden cage, suspended in a narrow hole by a rope and pulley. I could sit up, but the cage was too short to stand in. Torch light burned around the top of the hole. Mere inches below me, I saw the tips of long, wooden spikes with the bones of unlucky men scattered about them. My head ached, but I could feel that the skin wasn't broken.

The captain stepped to the edge of the hole to look down on me. Her hands rested on my sword hilts.

She had them fastened around her waist. Before I could say a word, she held her hands out and smiled. "Pirate," she reminded me.

"Those aren't to toy with, my dear," I warned.

"They're nice," she commented, unsheathing one. "But I'd much rather toy with you," she teased, smacking the rope that held my cage with the side of the blade, causing the cage to jostle.

I held on to the wooden bars and looked down at the spikes that awaited me.

"I'm not a bad girl. Oh wait, yes I am," she laughed. "I'm just suspicious of strangers—especially Dark Elf strangers—who show up at my restaurant. I have to look after my crew, you know."

"I told you already, I was caught in a storm. I'm not here to cause trouble. I'm not even sure where here is."

"And I'd like to keep it that way." She then walked away, leaving me caged in the hole.

"You can't keep me down here!" I yelled.

I heard her laugh in the distance. "You'll stay down there until I'm satisfied."

I then heard men sniggering from somewhere nearby. "Until she's satisfied," one of them mocked.

"Shut up!" Lorena yelled. "And get away from that hole."

"Sorry, Captain," they apologized and hurried away.

I didn't sit in my prison long before deciding it was time to escape. I slid my hand down one of the wooden bars and broke a splinter off in my hand. "Err!" I grunted. Once I removed the thick shard of wood, I squeezed drops of blood from the wound and focused my thoughts on the human bones resting at the bottom of the pit. Their flesh had fallen away, but I didn't need it to grant them movement again. Ethereal energy from an unseen plane began to materialize as a green aura that reconnected their bones like muscles. Organs took shape but had no function, and transparent skin covered their bodies, making the two skeletons appear like the ghosts of men who had died in that pit.

"Good evening, boys," I greeted them with a smile. "I'm glad you're here. Did you see what that human did to me?" I asked, pointing up and laughing. "Did she do the same to you?"

They didn't say a word, but they didn't have to. I could somehow draw memories from them as if reading their minds, even though their minds had long since gone black.

"Well, if you two would be so kind, I could use your assistance in escaping this cage."

The ghostly men scaled the muddy walls of the hole and began hoisting me up.

Just as my cage was lifted high enough for me to see out of the hole, I saw two of Lorena's men scrambling toward one of the huts that lined the bay. They began pounding their fists on the door and yelling, "Captain! Captain!" while looking back frightfully at the two spirits working to release me.

My cage was spun around to solid ground and the bottom unlatched, so I could escape. I snapped my fingers and pointed to the men trying to get Lorena to come outside. The two spirits ran up an embankment to them. The men immediately fell to their knees, surrendering. Lorena opened her door only long enough to see what was going on before voicing a humorous yelp and slamming the door shut.

"We're sorry! We're sorry! Please, don't kill us!" Lorena's men cried.

"Quiet!" I ordered them, walking up to the hut. "Come on out, Captain."

People in the surrounding huts peeped out their windows at what was happening but were too afraid to get involved.

"I'm sorry I imprisoned you," she apologized behind the door. "I wasn't going to leave you to die down there. It was only going to be for the night, so I could figure out what to do with you."

"She speaks the truth," one of her men said to me. "We weren't going to leave you down there, honest."

"Return my swords, and I'll return your men," I proposed.

"Unharmed?" the men asked fearfully while still on their knees at the feet of the undead.

I laughed. "Yes, all of you will be unharmed."

"Keep them," Lorena told me. "I have plenty of men. I'll get more use out of these swords than those two."

"NO! Captain, don't trade us," the men cried.

"Hand over my swords peacefully and keep your men, or I'll send my men in to take my swords by force," I told her with a laugh. I hoped she would refuse the deal, so I could give her a good scare.

My captives struggled to hold back their cries while they waited for their captain to make a decision.

She opened the door quickly, pointing one of the swords at my throat, but I didn't flinch. "Aren't you afraid I'll kill you like I did those two phantoms by your side?"

Calmly, I answered, "The skin is deceiving, but the dead tell know lies. You didn't kill these men, and I don't believe you'll kill me."

She sighed and sheathed the sword before handing them over to me. "You're right," she laughed at herself, shaking her head. "My father was the real pirate. I'm just a simple ship captain. I'm sorry. How's your head?"

"You gave me quite a headache," I answered, strapping the swords on my back.

"Well, I thought you were a pirate. And if there's anything I learned from my father, it's you can never trust a pirate."

"Can we go, now?" Lorena's frightened men begged.

"Go on, you crybabies," she told them, and they scrambled to their huts for the night.

"You too," I commanded the two dead men who released me from my cage. "And thank you."

One ran down the sandy bank and fell into the pit where I found him. The other moved closer, staring at me. The green ethereal muscles moved his jaw as if he tried to say something, but there was no sound.

"I know you don't have eyes," I responded, grabbing hold of his shoulders and turning him around. "Why don't you go do something?" I then pushed him away, and he scuffled after the other skeleton, falling into the pit.

It was well after midnight, and people were leaving the restaurant. There were many small huts built along the bay where they coupled up for the night.

I nodded to the captain and left to go sit on the

steps leading down to the dock. The ocean was quiet there in the bay. Looking up at the twinkling starlight, I instinctively reached for Jinxie's hand, but she wasn't there to take it. Instead, I felt a bottle pushed into it.

"You look like you can use a drink," Lorena said, taking a seat next to me. In her other hand, she held a smoking pipe.

I wiped the tears from my eyes and sniffed the bottle's contents. I turned it up, taking a long drink of the red wine. "Is this how you make friends; knock them out, throw them in a cage, and then offer them a fermented drink?"

"Why? Is it working?"

"No," I laughed, lightly touching my bruised face.

"So what was her name?"

"Excuse me?" her question catching me by surprise.

"The woman you're thinking about."

"I didn't know humans could read minds."

"It's always about women," she explained. "Or men, if you fancy that sort of thing."

"I don't want to talk about it," I told her, shaking my head before taking another drink of the wine she had brought me.

"Come now, don't lock up on me," she said, bumping her shoulder into me. She put her fingers under the bottle of wine I was holding and lifted it a few inches. "Perhaps you just need to drink a little more," she suggested.

I stayed tight-lipped, turning my eyes back to the stars.

"Do you know what I see when I look up there?"

she asked, turning her questions toward herself in hopes I'll soon talk.

I waited for an answer while she smoked her pipe. Looking up at the night sky, her blonde tresses fell past her shoulders. She exhaled a puff of smoke before revealing what her human eyes saw.

"I see a dark curtain, punctured by arrows and pricked by spears, allowing the light of Valhalla to shine through, assuring valiant warriors of the glorious battles that wait beyond."

"Wow! Now that sounds like an exciting place," I told her, impressed by her words.

Handing me her smoking pipe, she asked, "What is it that you see?"

I placed the pipe between my lips and let the smoke circulate my nasal passages before answering. "I see eternity. I see loneliness. I feel insignificant beneath the vastness of space."

"Then this is your chance to take a new direction. If there was anything I learned from my father, it was everyone around you and all those who came before you serve as an example of what you can be. Take what you can from them to better yourself and move on." She took a swallow of wine and sat the bottle between us. "So how are you planning to get home?"

"I no longer have a home," I answered quickly. My eyes filled with tears, and I looked away for a moment to calm myself.

Lorena placed a comforting hand on my shoulder to express her sorrow. "My father was a ship captain. He built this place, and my mother managed it."

"Where are they now?"

"My father died in battle, and disease took my

mother. Life out here is tough."

"Oh, I'm sorry to hear that."

She accepted my apology with a nod. "So what about your folks? I'm sure elves have parents, too."

"I miss my pop," I answered, remembering him teaching me the fundamentals of magic.

Lorena handed me the bottle of wine, so I took a swallow. "Has he passed on, too?" she asked, hesitantly.

I nodded and looked out at the ship tied to the pier. "He told me I should leave Ashwood. That was over a century ago."

"You're over a hundred years old?" Lorena coughed. "Give me that wine," she ordered, taking it from my hand.

She brought a much needed laugh from me. "I'm actually over two hundred years old, but who's counting?"

She began coughing and sat the bottle down to cover her mouth; she had become strangled on a swallow of wine.

I took hold of her wrist and lifted it. "Put your arm up," I told her.

She coughed out a laugh and pulled her arm away from me. "Stop it! You're crazy," she laughed. "How is lifting your arm supposed to help that?"

"Well, you're not strangled anymore."

"HA! You're a strange man, Ambros."

With a sly smile, I told her, "You haven't seen strange, yet."

"Then show me. What more can you do besides raise the dead? Show me the strangeness of elves," she teased, leaning into me. Her blue eyes gleamed in the torch light that lined the wooden walkway.

I laughed shyly. "Perhaps another time."

"Well, then let me see these beautiful swords again," she said, touching the sheaths still on my back. "I promise not to run off with them. Were they made by elves?"

"Pop made them." I reached behind my shoulders and unsheathed them. The two feet long obsidian blades burned with a subtle, mystical fire.

"They're pretty," she commented, reaching out to take them.

I handed her the black sword first. "This one is named Devour. And this one is Scourge," I said, handing her the green sword.

"I like the names; they make them sound scary." She held them out, feeling their weight. "Why do they glow like that? Are they magical?"

"Devour burns through all the moisture of whatever you cut with it. And where it attacks the body, Scourge attacks the mind," I described, tapping on my head. "It brings madness to a sane mind, dredging up an overwhelming flood of emotions. That is, if your enemy survives the wound it leaves."

Lorena's eyes were wide from my description. "They are scary. I want one."

"HAHAHAA!" I laughed.

Examining the blades closer, she asked, "What are they made of?"

"The blades are fashioned from a volcanic glass called obsidian."

"Glass? Wouldn't they shatter as soon as you strike something?"

"Well, it's more of a crystal," I explained. "It's already quite strong but strengthened by magic to be nearly unbreakable."

Handing my swords back to me, she asked, "So your father sent you away from home. Why?"

I sheathed my swords and exhaled heavily, thinking back to our last moments together. "Pop told me that his body would soon die, but we will be together again someday. He said that I would be killed and the city destroyed, so I was to leave Ashwood to stay with our cousins, the Light Elves."

"And was your city destroyed?"

I thought for a moment, remembering Kronyx saying he spoke with the new guardian of Ashwood. "No."

"Then you should go back. You should go home. If the city still stands, then your father's grim vision didn't come to pass."

"I have never known Pop to be wrong, no matter how bizarre or vague his visions were."

"Then you can still warn your people!" she exclaimed. "He may have told you to leave, but he didn't tell you that you couldn't go back."

"Pop said that only together can we save our people."

Lorena looked confused as she tried to understand what even I could not. "So you're just supposed to turn your back on your people?" she finally asked.

"I… I need some sleep," I told her, slowly getting to my feet. "Thank you for the drink."

I turned to walk up the stairs from the dock when she took hold of my hand. I jerked my hand away. "Only Jinxie may hold my hand," I said before realizing my rudeness. "I'm sorry…"

Sadly, Lorena whispered, "So that was her name."

I left to find a place to sleep in the forest; if I could sleep after all that's happened, after all that I've lost.

"Rain is coming," I heard her say behind me.

"Rain is coming," I repeated under my breath just as tears welled up in my eyes and broke from the edge of my lashes to pour down my face.

I walked between the huts and into the forest. I had to continually wipe tears from my eyes so that I could see where I was walking. The forest was sparse, and the sandy soil kept most of the undergrowth from taking root. Still within view of the restaurant, I took the pair of swords off my back and sat at the foot of a tree. I took a pinch of Jinxie's ashes from the pouch on my belt to examine and feel between my fingers.

"This is far beyond my power," I whispered to myself. "You were supposed to help me."

I laid down just as rain droplets began pelting the tree leaves above me. I began getting wet but didn't move from beneath the tree. Visions of my beloved Jinxie flooded my mind. I remembered her lying next to me, holding my hand while we drifted off to sleep, as she had done for decades but no more. She was gone, and I found myself holding my own hand. My hand tightened into a fist, and I beat the sand as the pain overwhelmed me. I wanted to be a kid again and free from the weight of the world. I wanted to be home in Lylandria with Jinxie in my arms. I wanted Pop here to assure me that everything was wonderful. But I couldn't have those things back. The life I lived was over.

It began raining harder, and the tree that I was

under could no longer keep me dry. I sat up from the dampening sand and pulled my knees up to my chest.

Jinxie's final act of bravery was to save me. She died so that I may live. The pain was unbearable, but I could not give up; the world needed me; my people needed me. Jinxie's sacrifice would not be in vain.

"Perhaps this was the best way you could help; you know I'll find a way to save you."

Through the trees, I saw Lorena running between the huts to come find me in the forest.

"Ambros! Ambros!" she called.

I stood from under the tree, and she hurried over to me.

She yelled over the pouring rain. "You can't rest out here in this. Come on."

I nodded, and she took hold of my wrist. We ran through the rain back to her hut where she had a fire burning inside for us to sit by.

The walls of the hut were made of bamboo that had been tied tightly together. The floor was soft sand, and the roof was made up of several layers of dried foliage over a bamboo frame. Wood panels were closed over the windows to keep the rain from blowing in. A small hatch near the roof's peak was open to allow smoke from the fire to escape.

Colorful hats and sharp weapons decorated the walls of her spacious hut. Against the left wall, a bed covered in furs sat atop a wooden platform. Firewood was neatly stacked to the right. At the back were several chests, a table, and a mirror.

Lorena grabbed a towel to wrap her wet hair in and tossed me one to use. "Feel free to strip down," she said, turning away from me.

Calling her out, I pointed to her reflection, "But you can still see me in the mirror!"

"All right," she laughed, holding her hands out. "You caught me."

Thinking for a moment, I suggested, "How about we sit in these chairs back to back by the fire and then we can both dry off with some privacy?"

Twisting her lips as she considered it, "That doesn't sound fun at all, but okay."

She grabbed another towel from a table and a robe for herself, and we turned our chairs so we could sit back to back.

I dried my hair with the towel and unbuttoned my black shirt, tossing it into the fire. It immediately vanished into the magical realm from whence I had summoned it.

"Hey! Don't you think you'll want to put those back on in the morning?" she asked.

I turned my head to see her speaking over her bare shoulder. To show her that I could easily recreate my clothing, I held my hands out to the side so she could watch me magically pull a hair ribbon from my hand.

"Did you make that?" Lorena asked, reaching back to take the ribbon.

"Magic isn't used just for destruction or raising the dead. It can also be used to create." I pulled off my shoes and tossed them, too, in the fire to see them immediately dissipate.

"So you make your own clothing from magic?"

"I do," I answered, removing my pants. I threw them into the fire and used the towel she had given me to dry off.

"Can you make rope?"

"I can, but like all summoned materials, it doesn't retain its strength for very long. The rope will unravel and dissipate after a few hours unless it's maintained."

"Well, I suppose you can always use it to tie me up," she whispered seductively.

I hurried to clothe myself, concentrating on another pair of pants. A light smoke swirled around my ankles and worked its way up my legs as it created a dark fabric. I summoned another shirt the same way before noticing that Lorena was no longer behind me. Turning around in my chair, I saw that she had turned her chair, so she could watch me. I suddenly felt embarrassed.

"There's no reason to be shy. I didn't see anything that I shouldn't," she smiled.

Wearing a fine silk robe, she sat with her legs crossed and one arm draped casually over the back of her chair. Her hair was brushed neatly straight, and her sun kissed skin looked luxurious in the fire light. I couldn't deny that she was beautiful, well, for a human. And it wasn't just her physical features that made her attractive. It was the way she carried herself, her take-charge attitude, her unhindered nature.

Realizing that I had been studying her for too long, I looked around the room. "So where should I sleep tonight?" I finally asked.

Nodding to the bed, Lorena answered, "Well, we could share the bed, or I can sleep here in this chair."

"I would prefer to sleep alone," I answered quickly, "but I cannot take your bed. I'll sleep here in the chair."

"You're my guest. I don't mind giving you the

bed for one night. I insist that you sleep in it. After what you've told me, you could use a good night's rest."

Giving in to her hospitality, I accepted the offer to sleep in the comfortable looking bed of thick animal furs. I stepped up on the platform and sat on the edge of the bed, pulling several layers of furs back. I placed my swords under the covers in case she felt the desire to steal them again.

"So you've chosen to sleep with your swords instead of a woman? I like you more and more," she commented, drawing a tired laugh from me.

"Thank you for giving me a place to sleep for the night." My body seemed to melt beneath the warm furs, and my eyes fell shut. The sound of pouring rain and burning wood eased me to sleep.

CHAPTER V

THE CRIMSON SPEAR

Dawn came, and the rain had passed. A warm breeze blew in through the open shutters, and Lorena was singing softly. "Ugh, I'm alive," I grunted, sitting up on my elbow and rubbing my face. "Good morning," Lorena said cheerfully. She was already dressed and looking at herself in the mirror while she brushed her hair. She took a sip from a mug and walked over to a kettle on the fire to dip out a cup for me.

I found my swords that were still in the bed with me and sat by the fire with her. Looking at the thick, red liquid within the mug that she handed me, I asked, "No spoon?"

She took a spoon from a pot of utensils near her and handed it to me.

Dipping it into the steaming cup, I found nothing solid within it to eat. "There's nothing in it!" I declared.

"There's not supposed to be anything in it; it's tomato soup, silly."

I held it to my nose to sniff, and Lorena laughed at me.

"Hmm, okay." I handed the spoon back to her and took a sip of the soup. Smacking my lips as I tasted it, I nodded to her. "Not bad. Thank you."

While sitting by the fire drinking soup, I thought about where to go from there. I needed answers. I needed to go back to Ashwood and meet their dragon guardian. Perhaps then I could find out what happened to Magnus and why pop put so much faith in him.

After finishing her cup of soup, Lorena poured a kettle of water over the fire to put it out. "Come on. I'm ready for some breakfast."

"You mean, this is not it?"

She waved for me to follow her, and we walked back to her restaurant where people were already eating.

With mouths full of food, everyone she walked by saluted her with a muffled, "Mornin', Captain."

She gave only a respectful nod as she headed toward the breakfast buffet.

Like the night before, a long table was filled with fruit, freshly baked breads, and many different types of seafood. I followed Lorena around the table while we filled our plates. She picked up a stick that had grilled chunks of fruit and curled pieces of meat on it. She placed one on both our plates. "You have to try this."

"What is it?"

"It is skewered shrimp and pineapple," she

answered as she headed to an empty table. "It's delight-ful."

I sat across from her and began sampling the food on my plate.

"So how do you like it?" she asked while she ate.

I had to turn away; seeing her eat was making me nauseous. I had dissected maggot-filled carcasses on hot summer days with hardly a cough, but this human was turning my stomach just by eating breakfast. She was like a reanimated deer, beautiful, yet vicious.

"That good, huh?" she commented when I didn't answer her.

When I looked back at her, I saw a corpse pulling shrimp from a skewer with its teeth! It had stringy, blonde hair and wore the same clothes that Lorena had been wearing. It was indeed Captain Lorena, only I saw her as a corpse. I closed my eyes and tried to shake away the vision.

"Are you okay?" she asked, reaching across the table to touch my hand.

I pulled my hand away and looked around the room to remind myself where I was but saw everyone as corpses! I examined my hands and found them to look healthy. I had skin, but everyone else was rotting.

"Ambros! Are you okay?" she repeated.

Looking back to her, she appeared normal. I took a deep breath and tapped a finger on the side of my head. "Death and decay rots away the brain."

"You scare me sometimes, you know that?"

"HA! I scare you? If only you saw the world as I see it," I told her as I began to eat my breakfast.

"And how do you see the world?" she asked with a smile.

"Everything is dead." My expression was as lifeless as my words. "You're dead." I pointed to a grizzled old man at the table next to us. "He's dead." I pointed to the ladies putting food out on the buffet. "They're dead. Everyone in here, everyone I've ever met, everyone I expect to meet is dead. And we eat the dead," I added, lifting my plate on one side. "But what I can't understand," I said, looking at my hands, "is how come I look alive?"

The old man sitting at the table next to us stood up and said, "You're scaring me." He began to leave but came back for his bacon. He then walked out of the restaurant.

"I could have sworn I was alive when I woke up this morning," Lorena joked.

"I wish I knew what was wrong with me."

"Is there anyone back home you could talk to? Do you have friends there?"

Staring at the food on my plate, I shook my head. Then I remembered Pop's notes and how he created me. A spark of hope lit my face. "Well, there may be something. Do you think you can take me home?"

Lorena burped and wiped her mouth on her sleeve before answering. "I don't know. Any place from here is a long journey."

"Okay, what do you want?"

Pointing to the swords on my back, she answered, "Devour would be nice."

"These were given to me by my pop..."

"These were given to me by my pop," she mocked. "You asked what I wanted, so I told you. You have nothing else to barter with." She then bit her lip and started to suggest another form of payment. "We could..."

"...get you a similar sword once we reach Ashwood," I said before she could say what I believed she was about to suggest.

Lorena laughed and took a bite of bread. "Ready the Spear," she ordered loudly to everyone in the restaurant. The men immediately left their tables and hurried out the door.

"How many men does it take?" I asked.

Lorena went about finishing her breakfast. "Go ahead and finish your meal," she answered between bites.

While I ate, I watched women clear tables and put away food. Lorena ate much quicker than I did, so she handed her empty plate to one of the ladies and got her mug refilled with juice to drink.

Once I finished, she downed the last of her juice and motioned for me to follow her outside where she pointed to the ship in the bay. "That is my ship, the Crimson Spear. It belonged to my father, but the other ship captains that sail these waters know that I didn't follow in his nefarious footprints. Where he deceived people to obtain goods, I try to build and maintain business relations through bartering."

The ship was narrow and painted red. It tapered into a point at the front and had a platform built at the rear, or what the sailors called the bow and stern of the ship.

Men loaded crates aboard the ship while women carried on baskets of food and jugs of water. We walked out on the pier and stepped over onto the ship. A couple dozen men sat on boxes along the deck where they readied long oars to propel it.

I followed Lorena into a small room beneath the ship's rear platform where she unrolled a map on a table. "Show me where you need to go, and I'll get you there," she told me, and I pointed to the place.

When everyone was ready, Captain Lorena gave the order to depart, and the ship was slowly paddled out of the bay and out to sea.

I was a child of the forest, so I felt vulnerable, yet free, in the open waters. The salty ocean air was refreshing. A large flock of birds rested on the waves, paying no mind as we passed by.

The women braided each other's hair to keep from getting tangles. Lorena offered me a hat to protect my head from the harsh sun, but I told her that elves do not sunburn.

As the men began to sweat from rowing, the women wiped their brows and brought them water.

"Who do you work for?" Lorena yelled at the men.

"Captain Lorena!" they all answered in unison, rowing harder.

"What do you work for?" Lorena asked them.

"Legs and tail!"

Walking between the rows of men, she asked, "And who has the hottest legs and tail of them all?"

"Captain Lorena!"

"That's right!" she proclaimed, placing a sandaled foot on one of the men's back as he rowed. "Now do my bidding and push! Pull! Harder! Faster!" She repeated the orders over and over to keep them in rhythm. "We've broken through the current and have a good wind," she announced to her crew. "Raise the sail!"

The men quickly pulled in their oars and hoisted a single white sail depicting a bloody spear. With the wind to our backs, Lorena stepped up on the rear platform and took over the steering oar from one of her female crewmates. She steered the ship while her crew filled their mugs to celebrate. One of the crew members began lightly stamping his feet. Others joined in, and the beat grew louder. Once everyone was stamping out the beat, they began singing.

> With our ship in the sea,
> The wind in our sail,
> And ale in our mugs,
> We are free!

> With our gods in the sky,
> The world at our feet,
> And stars as our guide,
> We're alive!

The crew began repeating the lyrics, and a pretty, red-haired lady took my hand, pulling me into the fun. I mimicked her movements, stamping my feet and thrusting a fist into the air. I saw Lorena at the rear of the ship laughing and clapping her hands with the beat, happy to see me included.

After the celebration died down, everyone returned to their duties of weaving rope and working on other necessities. I walked to the back to talk to Lorena while she steered the ship.

"I see you survived a round with my crew," she said to me while looking across the ship to the distant horizon.

"I must admit, I had fun," I nodded.

"Well, don't you start making a habit of having fun," she joked, shaking a finger at me.

I retrieved a stool from the cabin and carried it up to the platform to sit on, but Lorena sat on it instead. "Thank you, darling," she said, taking her hat off for a moment to wipe the sweat from her brow. "Piper," she called for her first mate to bring her a drink and to take the steering oar.

The red-haired woman who sang and danced with me brought water and took the oar.

"So, how much longer will we be out here?" I asked Lorena, sitting on a corner of her crate.

She laughed. "Sweetie, we're going to be out here a week."

"A wink?" Looking around, I asked, "Then where's land?"

"A week!" she corrected harshly.

"A week!" I repeated, shocked that it would take so long.

"Yes. Meaning seven days. Did you want my help getting home or not?"

"I do need your help," I answered. "And I am grateful for all you're doing. Without a dragon to ride, I wouldn't have gotten very far on my own."

The entire crew suddenly became nervous and scanned the surroundings, searching the sky and over the side of the boat.

Lorena shook her head. "Don't say that word," she whispered. "The ocean may appear safe, but you can't let your guard down. My father told me that, long ago, giants ruled these waters. None have been seen for many a year, but we still hear tales of terrible serpents destroying entire fleets from beneath the waves."

"Have you never seen one?"

"No." Leaning in close, she whispered, "But I'd like to . . . just not at sea."

"Be careful what you wish for," I warned. "They are vile, scheming creatures, and no doubt just as dangerous at sea as they are on land."

"And you have ridden one?" she asked in disbelief.

"A dead one," I boasted with a laugh.

She was speechless.

My laughter quickly faded as I remembered what the dead dragon took from me in life.

"Walk with me to the bow," she said, taking my hand.

The warm sun felt wonderful against my skin. Memories of running hand in hand with Jinxie on bright summer days came back to me.

Lorena breathed in deeply and stretched in the afternoon sun. "Have you ever seen a more peaceful view?" she asked, staring out at the ocean meeting the sky.

"I have, but this is nice, too."

Turning to me, she asked, "Tell me about where you're from."

"Well, I was born in the Dark Elf city of Ashwood. It was built within a volcano under a roof of obsidian. Combining magic with what little sunlight filtered in from above and the heat that emanated from below made it possible for us to grow plants and trees. After Pop's death, I left Ashwood to live with the Light Elves of Lylandria. It was a vast garden that was always in bloom. I spent many days lying under fruit trees with

Jinxie watching the sun rise and set."

"Sounds wonderful."

"Were you close to your family?" I asked.

"I was close to my mother. All I learned from my father was how not to be. But enough about that," she said, slapping her thighs. "I believe I've had a long enough break."

I followed her to the stern where she took over steering. Piper, Lorena's first mate, joined the rest of the crew in preparing the evening meal. They had a tripod where two pots hung. The bottom pot was the largest and held wood that they ignited. It heated the pot of stew that hung above it.

After the sun sank into the sea and darkness fell upon the ship, everyone but Lorena sat around the tripod to eat dinner. She made sure the ship stayed on course. Her first mate would take over later to let Lorena eat and get a few hours of sleep.

Piper dipped out a bowl of stew for me. Stirring to allow it to cool before taking a bite, I saw that it had bits of seafood and vegetables in it.

Being the odd one among the crew, I was asked to share my story, and what a story I told. Everyone was captivated by my tale and wondered what I planned to do once I reached Ashwood.

"I want to create life," I answered.

"Only the gods have that power," one of the men told me. I knew he was young, but he had clearly lived a hard life out there on the sea; they all had. All of Lorena's men were strong, swarthy, and calloused.

Believing the Sun to be both our god and paradise, I asked, "And what do your gods do exactly?"

"They keep everything in balance," another

sailor explained. He held his hands out like a set of scales but struggled to maintain balance. He gave examples, "Like good and evil, light and dark, life and death."

"Drunk and sober," another man added, holding his drink up but spilling some on the man sitting next to him.

"Dry and wet," he complained, wiping the mead from his arm.

"Beauty and the beast," Piper added, pointing from herself to the drunken sailor.

The man looked shocked. "Hey! Last night, you said I was the beauty and you were the beast."

"Well, Sal, that's because you were wearing my clothes," she revealed, striking a provocative pose, which brought laughs and whistles from everyone.

Even Sal laughed, remembering the previous night. "It was fun, Pipes. You were definitely a beast," he said, biting at her.

She grabbed his jaw and pulled him close for a kiss. The rest of the crew cheered. She then strolled to the stern to relieve Lorena.

The captain joined us around the fire, but at that late hour, the crew was ready to lie down for the evening. They unrolled mats on the deck and slept under the stars.

The next day played out the same; the crew sang and danced, drank mead, and told tales. That night, though, my eyes opened suddenly, for uneasiness crept over me. Vibrations of light footsteps passed through the ship, and the ocean air carried the scent of death. I reached over to shake Lorena awake and saw a strange man pull the curtain of the captain's quarters back. He slipped inside with a dagger in hand. I unsheathed one of my swords, and sliced him across the wrist, causing him to drop his blade before he could kill Lorena. The man screamed and ran out of the room, waking the crew from their sleep.

"A demon sails with them!" the man cried. "There's a demon in the darkness!" he yelled at one of his fellow assassins before taking the man overboard with him.

Hooks were thrown into our ship, and men on another ship pulled the two together.

"Kill those pirates!" I heard the captain of the other ship order his crew.

Looking at Lorena, I said, "But I thought they were the pirates."

"Um, they are," she answered hesitantly. "Kill them! It's us or them."

Four members of her crew didn't stir from their slumber, so I knew right away that they had been killed in their sleep. We needed all the help we could get, so I gave them life again. By sending a thought to their dead mind, I ignited a spark to get them moving again and follow my command.

"These men killed you while you slept," I informed them. "Now they mean to kill your friends. Send them to the bottom of the ocean."

The four zombies unsheathed their daggers and charged toward their nearest adversary. After dying from a simple knife wound to the chest, they looked to be healthy sailors, so the pirates they fought were surprised to see them unharmed by their attacks.

After one zombie was slashed across the throat, it sliced the pirate's belly and kicked him overboard.

"That-a-boy!" I congratulated. I remained close to Lorena to help protect her from the pirates. Every man we killed, I brought back to help us. It wasn't long before our crew outnumbered the other, and being at sea, they had nowhere to run.

The captain of the other ship fought his way over to our ship with a sword and spear. He was a hulk of a man wearing mismatched pieces of brightly painted armor. His skin was dark from life in the sun, and the brown hair on his head grew sparsely around horrible scars.

The man battled his way to us. "Hello, bitch!" the muscular man greeted Lorena, his bare arms covered in the blood of her crew. "I guess if you want a ship captain dead, you have to kill them yourself."

"I couldn't have said it better myself," I responded as I sliced off the head of his spear when he lunged at Lorena.

"Outta my way, you lil' shit," the big man said before cracking me across the face with what was left of his spear and kicking me over a wooden crate.

"I should've killed you while you slept, Maddox," I heard Lorena tell him as I struggled to regain my balance.

"And I should have sank your treacherous ass in the ocean for stealing my ship, you pirate wench."

Lorena stumbled backwards to avoid the man's powerful attacks, and I hurried to intervene. I swung at him, but he used his sword to deflect mine. He swung the shaft of his spear, but I cut it even shorter. While I had his attention, Lorena climbed over a crate that she was using to keep distance between them and stabbed him in the neck with her dagger.

With the bronze dagger embedded at the base of his neck, Maddox backhanded Lorena away and slowly collapsed to the deck of the ship. "I'll hunt for you in the next life," he sputtered, struggling to look up at Lorena.

"What, you going to try killing me again?" she asked him, retrieving her dagger from his neck. Blood poured from the wound, and the man said no more.

I'd seen and studied death my entire life, but as I stood there, staring down at this now lifeless man, I wondered why the world couldn't be perfect and peaceful. Why did Lorena feel she needed to lie to me about how she acquired the ship we sailed on? What kind of life did Maddox live to think killing Lorena and her crew was the only way to retrieve his stolen ship?

After the chaos, we took a headcount of who survived. Half of Lorena's crew had been killed. I looked around at the zombies I had created. They were alive just moments earlier. There would be no reason for war if everyone were immortal.

"Where's Pipes?" I heard Sal ask while he searched the ship. "She was at the helm!" he reminded himself and pushed passed the standing dead to the stern. "PIPES! NO!"

Lorena and I rushed to the stern to find Sal hugging Piper's dead body.

"Oh, Piper," Lorena cried.

"Will you heal her, elf?" Sal asked me.

"I'm sorry. If I bring her back, she will be mindless. She will be undead."

"Don't bring her back," Lorena shook her head, heartbroken. "I'm sorry, Sal. I loved her, too." She placed a comforting hand on his shoulder.

Sal pulled his dead love close and sobbed. Piper's throat had been cut. No doubt, she was the first to be killed by the pirates when they quietly climbed aboard.

The living crew members all gathered around to bury Piper at sea. I drew a magical shroud from an unseen realm for them to wrap her in, and they placed her into the dark ocean waters where she sank out of sight.

Lorena removed her hat before beginning her eulogy. "We lost a lot tonight. We didn't just lose our crewmates, we lost our friends, but they've sailed on to a better place. We miss them now, but we will see them again," her voice took on a more hopeful tone as she looked up to the night sky.

The remaining crewmembers stood silent for a moment until Sal asked his captain what their orders were.

Lorena put her hat back on while staring down at the wooden planks of the ship. "It will be difficult, but we must sail on."

"Excuse me, Captain," I interjected. "My men can help sail this vessel."

She looked around at all the dead I had brought back, and a smile cracked across her face. "Then I want both ships!" she announced. "Sal, I'm promoting you to Captain. Take the crew to sail our new ship."

He stared off knowing that Piper would have been the one promoted had she lived.

"Captain Salvatore!" she stressed, bringing him to attention. "I want to know the cargo we've acquired before we detach."

"Yes, Captain Lorena," he finally answered. He

then motioned to the sailors to join him.

"And Captain?"

Sal turned back to her with a tear trickling down his cheek, his lips pressed tightly to keep them from quivering.

"We sail on for Piper," Lorena announced, nearly breaking again under their loss.

Wiping the tear from his face, he nodded and stepped over to the other ship.

"All right, line up!" I commanded my zombie soldiers, and they all scuffled over to stand in semi-straight lines. There were a lot, probably as many as fifty. I divided them between the two ships to man the oars, and after Captain Salvatore returned with a cargo manifest, we unhooked the ropes that bound our ships together and continued our journey.

Once I felt comfortable commanding zombie pirates to do the jobs they did in life, I had them begin stamping out the rhythm to the song we sang just after setting sail to try lightening the mood. I stood on a wooden crate, and, as if conducting an orchestra, I waved my arms about, keeping the zombies of both ships synchronized in work and song. Of course, only I could interpret the grunts and groans that they spat, but the bizarre show entertained the living as I had hoped.

With all the zombies working closely with Lorena and her crewmen, I was careful not to fall asleep. Of course, she didn't sleep at all with a crew of decomposing sailors aboard her ship, so we helped each other stay awake by asking questions and telling stories.

After several more days at sea, we reached a bustling city built between the ocean and mountains. It was a sunny afternoon with clear skies and sparkling blue waters.

Removing her smoking pipe to speak, Lorena announced, "The port city of Genua." She navigated the Crimson Spear through the busy waters with Sal's ship following closely. Ships of all sizes inhabited the harbor where we slowly sailed in to dock.

To avoid a zombie outbreak, like the one that happened at the World Council Palace, I felt it best to go ahead and retrieve the spark of life from the zombie sailors. One at a time, they stepped over the edge of the ship to sink to the bottom of the bay.

Lorena removed her hat, followed by the rest of her crew, and said a few words in honor of the fallen. "You were all brave sailors. We couldn't have asked for better crewmates or better drinking buddies. I'm sure Piper captains a mighty vessel off the golden shores of Valhalla," she announced with a proud smile, her blonde curls blowing in the wind. "Now she has the finest crew to sail those magnificent waters. We miss you, but we'll sail together again someday."

A wide plank was placed to bridge the boat to the pier, and the crew unloaded six heavy crates from the Crimson Spear to carry into the city. They used long wooden poles to distribute the weight evenly between the two men it took to carry one.

"What's with all the crates?" I asked sleepily.

"Before we trek out into the wilderness, we'll need a few supplies," Lorena said to me. "Most will go back with us to the restaurant. You and I will carry what we need north to your homeland."

While the crew worked, Lorena and I took a much-needed nap before leaving the ship. I pulled at the collar of my black tunic. The material formed a hood to help hide my elvish features.

The crew followed us across the pier and along the harbor through the crowd of people to a shop with an adjacent horse stable. Wooden cages filled with chickens were stacked on both sides of the entrance. A dark-skinned man with a neatly trimmed beard leaning in the entryway smiled at the sight of us.

"Capitan Lorena," he greeted with a delightful accent, his arms outstretched to hug her. "It is so wonderful to see you again, my dear."

"How've you been, Enzo?" she asked him, clearly glad to see him, as well.

"Fantastico! Fantastico!" He then took notice of me, and saw that I wasn't human beneath my dark hood.

"He's good," Lorena assured him, answering his unasked question. "He's with me."

He accepted her answer and continued. "Now, what is it that Enzo can do for the lovely Lorena?"

Turning to the six crates that her men carried with them, she told the gentleman, "I brought the cargo you requested."

"Very good. Bring them around back, and we'll have a look, shall we?"

Lorena signaled to her crew to carry the crates between the buildings to the back of the shop while we followed Enzo inside.

The thick, clay walls of the building kept it cool inside regardless of how hot it became outside, which was good for keeping the variety of fruits and vegetables that he had for sale from spoiling too quickly. A young boy was busy rotating stock.

"Watch the store for a moment," Enzo said to the boy, patting him on the shoulder as he passed.

Lorena grabbed a couple of peaches from a basket and tossed me one while we followed Enzo through his shop. We stepped out the back door where several other crates were stacked. Lorena's men had already opened the shipment for Enzo to inspect the contents. The back wall of another building gave us privacy from the street.

Looking into the crates, I saw they were full of shields, swords, and short spears. Enzo lifted a shield to examine the thickness of the wood it was made from. He felt the sharpness of a sword and the durability of a spear before approving the shipment. "I will have your payment and cargo packed up and ready to go tomorrow evening."

"Good," Lorena smiled. "I'll have my men pick it up." Rubbing the man's beard, she added, "And I could use a couple horses, if you have any to spare."

"Of course, my dear, but I only have one."

"It will do. You're a good man, Enzo. Thank you." She embraced the courteous man before we headed back to the ship for the evening.

CHAPTER VI

THE JOURNEY HOME

The following morning, Lorena said her good-byes to her crew.

"If I'm not back in three weeks, head home without me," she ordered Captain Salvatore.

"But Captain, why don't you take some of the men with you?" Sal suggested.

"Because you can't afford to lose any more experienced sailors," she answered sadly. "In my absence, you should recruit new men."

"Very well, Captain," Sal accepted with a sigh.

With a point of her finger and a grin on her face, she repeated, "Men, Sal. You'll never leave port if you bring too many women aboard."

Sal and the rest of the crew burst into laughter.

"Hey, you're the one who felt we should wait out a storm brewing off the coast, and then you got sick eating oysters at that bar," Sal reminded her.

I saw Lorena's stomach turn just thinking about it. She looked away and held a hand up to stop him from talking about it.

"You didn't expect us to just sit around and twiddle our thumbs, did you?" he added.

Lorena coughed to clear her throat. "But that wasn't all you twiddled."

Shaking his head, Sal argued, "Everything was fine until Felix and Hernando started fighting over that pretty, young thing. What was his name? Was it Lester?" he asked, looking to the sailors in question, trying his best to hold back chuckles.

"He told Felix it was Lesley," Hernando spoke up, already beginning to laugh.

Felix pointed to Hernando. "You knew she was a man!"

Through giggling laughter, Lorena asked him, "How long did it take you to find out she had a rudder?"

"While he was dropping anchor," Hernando answered for him, bringing everyone to tears.

"Take care of yourself out there, Captain," Sal told her, holding a fist head-high in the air, followed by the rest of the crew.

Lorena returned the salute with a fist in the air.

"Hurry on back, Captain" Hernando added. "You never know what trouble Felix may stir up in your absence."

"Just don't sink my ship," Lorena commanded, hanging a worn leather bag of supplies over her shoulder and stepping off the ship onto the pier.

"Bring some elf women back with you," we heard Felix say as we walked across the pier back to the city.

People were already hard at work loading and unloading ships with goods, and the markets were busy selling fresh foods and spices. We walked down to Enzo's store. He was brushing the mane of the horse we were to take on our journey.

"Thank you again for everything," Lorena said to him, kissing his cheek.

"Try not to get into too much trouble, my dear," he said before helping us load up the horse and sending us on our way.

We led the horse slowly through the busy streets. Further into the city, the air was rich with the aroma of foods being cooked at the many restaurants. We then passed by homes with kids playing outdoors before reaching the outer region of the city where people raised livestock.

"We should be able to acquire another horse at one of these farms," Lorena told me. "I brought enough money to purchase one."

I told her to save it. With no one around to frighten, I removed my hood to feel the sunlight on my face. I outstretched my hand and moved it slowly along in front of me.

"Ambros, are you okay?"

"Jackpot!" I said with a smile as the dirt started shifting at the edge of a field. The skeleton of a horse pulled itself from the earth and galloped over to us. "And what's your name, fella?" I asked the undead horse while I rubbed its bony face. I laughed at the name that I heard his master say resonating through his bones. "Ralph," I said aloud.

"I didn't hear it say anything."

Tapping on my head, I explained, "I heard it in here." I placed my hands against the ribs of the horse, and a thick material began forming to cover his sharp spine.

Lorena mounted her horse, but I stopped her from leaving just yet. "While we're here, I'd like to raise another that I sense nearby."

Another patch of dirt began to move, and Lorena asked, "What do we need with another horse?"

A boney hand protruded from the ground and pushed at the soil to free itself.

"Not a horse. A human," I clarified. "We need a watchman while we sleep, so we are not ambushed."

I commanded the human skeleton to rise from its grave, and the dusty collection of bones scuffled over for me to examine. With several broken ribs and a damaged skull, the individual clearly met a terrible end. I climbed on my skeletal horse to continue our journey. "Let's go, Ralph."

I trotted ahead before noticing that Lorena was lagging behind. She was purposely riding slower so the skeleton could keep up. I stopped and waited for them.

"So you're just going to make him run?" Her voice carried a tone of anger and guilt.

"Lorena, it's nothing but bones," I explained a bit colder than I meant to. "It can't get tired; magic holds it together, and magic fuels it."

The dead human stopped next to us and scanned the surroundings with its empty eye sockets.

"Then why use human remains at all? Why not gather some sticks and stones to cast your fancy magic on?"

"Because bones hold a kind of residual memory

that sticks and stones do not possess," I explained. "I don't have to direct every movement; they already know how to move. They just need the means to do so."

I rode on, but Lorena again fell behind, riding next to the skeleton.

"He's just going to slow us down," she argued. "Look at him."

I turned and politely said, "Lorena, my dear, she has been given the task to watch after you. You're the one slowing her down."

I regretted it as soon as I said it. I didn't mean to let slip that the skeleton I had raised was a woman in life. I thought Lorena carried enough sorrow with her already with the loss of her friend.

"She? What was her name?" Lorena asked sadly. "How did she die?"

"Her name was Mariana," I finally answered. "She was trampled by Ralph when he became spooked by wolves."

Teary-eyed, she stared at the dry, dusty skeleton standing next to us for a long moment. "Will you put some clothes on her?"

I got down from my horse and stepped up to the bare-bone corpse. I held my hand out for her to take, and she placed her boney hand in mine. I placed my other hand on top and looked into her eye sockets. A thick, black cloth began to form around her wrist and spread over her body to form a hooded robe to hide her naked deadness.

Lorena waited for me to get back on my skeletal horse, and she rode on. She's seen a lot of death the past few days, and I could tell it was weighing heavily on her.

Mariana ran along behind us, having no trouble keeping up as we continued on our journey down a well-worn road into a mountainous region. The only sound from her was the light thump of her boney feet meeting the dirt road.

After a long while of traveling in silence, Lorena asked, "You've been awfully quiet. What's on your mind?"

She was right. I, too, had a lot weighing on me. I was heading home to Ashwood, where I haven't been in well over a century. "I'm nervous. I'm not so sure if going back is a good idea."

"You're going to make sure your city still stands and find the answers to your questions. If you want answers, you have to go get them. They're not going to just fall in your lap like a drunken sailor," she explained. "Which reminds me…," she added as she reached behind her to retrieve a bottle of wine from the satchel on her horse. She pulled the cork with her teeth and took a drink. "You're making the right decision by going back."

"As far as I've heard, Ashwood still exists. I just hope pop's notes have endured all these years."

"Why didn't you take them when you left?"

"HA! You should have seen the amount of notes he had. There was no way I could carry them all. I took only what Pop instructed me to," my voice trailed off as I thought about why he didn't have me take his important notes.

Noticing that I was deep in thought, Lorena packed her wine away and asked, "What is it?"

"Maybe it's nothing, but I find it odd that he didn't send me with at least some of his notes."

"Well, it's not like he could see the future and know that you would be interested in them someday."

I laughed. "Actually, he could see into the future. There was reason behind everything he did."

"Then he must have seen you would return, and perhaps he knew it would be for his notes."

"Perhaps." I rubbed my chin, wondering just how clear his visions were.

We traveled at a steady pace the entire day. We talked about the warm sun and the crisp, fall breeze. We shared stories about our childhood. We discussed our religious beliefs. Lorena was noticeably sad about losing Piper and several other crewmates, but she was a strong woman for not letting it slow her down.

Upon reaching a narrow stream, we decided to camp for the night. We tied the horses to a tree at the water's edge and cleared an area where she started a fire. I closed my fingers loosely into fists and shook them in unison in front of me. A magical material formed to create a thick, white blanket. I spread the blanket out on the ground, and we sat next to each other where we could keep watch on the horses standing by the stream. I sent a silent command to Mariana to sit on a fallen tree and keep watch behind us. The sound from any approaching creature will resonate through Mariana's bones and will alert me of possible danger.

Lorena took her hat off that had been keeping the sun off her all day and uncorked her bottle of wine for another drink. She unbraided her thick, blonde locks, letting them fall over her shoulders. "You know, you have a very unique look."

"Thanks," I said emotionless, watching the burning wood of our campfire.

"No, I mean that in a good way," she laughed. She stared at me long enough to make me feel uncomfortable. "You have hair like fine silk, skin like a moonlit night, and eyes, eyes like the sun."

"Thank you," I smiled, finally looking at her. "That makes me feel good."

"You're welcome, hon," she said with a wink.

I walked over to the horses and looked into one of the satchels that Enzo had packed for us full of food. There were fruits, vegetables, and a couple loaves of bread. I took two stalks of celery and broke off a chunk of bread to divide with Lorena.

"What are you carrying in that little pouch?" she asked, pointing to it hanging from my belt.

Hesitantly, I answered, "A handful of my mate's ashes."

"Jinxie," she whispered sadly, remembering her name. "I'm sorry."

While shifting the burning wood of our campfire around with a stick, I told her what I hoped to accomplish in Ashwood besides warning them about the dragons' increasing power in the east and figuring out why I see living people as if they are dead. "Pop created me," I began. "I have no mother like everyone else. He grew me from his right eye in a vat of elixir that he concocted. After his death, I left Ashwood to live with the Light Elves of Lylandria where I met Jinxie. I was no one in Ashwood, but in Lylandria, I was someone. I was interesting because I was different. And Jinxie made me feel special every day that we were together."

"How'd she die?"

I was barely able to utter, "Dragon breath."

Lorena gasped. "Oh, Ambros, I'm so sorry."

"Her death pushes me to succeed."

"And will you?" she asked.

Doubting myself, I finally answered, "I must."

She put an arm around me and leaned her head against my shoulder to comfort me while we sat by the crackling fire.

We sat quietly together for a long while before her snores alerted me that she had fallen asleep on my shoulder. I quietly laughed at the nasally sounds she made as she slept before gently laying her on the blanket we had been sitting on. I created another blanket in the same manner to place over her and made a separate bed for myself.

It was quiet, except for the wind blowing dead leaves from the trees and the trickling of water breaking over rocks in the stream. I took a deep breath to relax and closed my eyes to sleep.

I had just gone to sleep when a sense of danger startled me. I threw the blanket off and got to my feet. The fire still burned, and Lorena still slept. Everything seemed to be fine. I hurried over to Mariana who was still sitting upon a log.

"WHAT?" I quietly yelled in the skeleton's face, so I wouldn't wake Lorena.

Mariana's mouth opened, and she raised a boney hand to point at a dung beetle that was making its way through the leaves toward the camp. I snatched it up and crushed it in my fist in front of her face. I threw it down and wiped my hand on the cloak that covered her shoulders. Returning to my bed by the fire, I went back to sleep.

I found myself under water. I knew I was dreaming, but I didn't try waking myself; I like exploring beyond the veil of sleep. I had no trouble breathing, but I couldn't tell which way was up and which was down. There was just enough light and pressure around me to tell I was surrounded by water. I chose a direction to swim, hoping to reach the surface or find bottom, so I would at least know which direction was up. As I swam, the dim light that illuminated the water stayed the same, growing neither lighter nor darker. I decided not to change course and kept swimming.

I felt as if I'd swum miles, but the brightness of the water looked the same—gloomy. I continued on and began to see a shape of someone in the distance. I hurried toward them. It was an elf! I opened my mouth to speak but water rushed in to silence my words. I pointed to him, to me, and then into the direction we should swim. He nodded, and we swam together, finding another elf alone in the water. The three of us swam, finding more and more elves. Some were alone and others were already grouped together in the dark waters. Among the crowd, I caught a glimpse of Jinxie! I swam quickly past everyone to get to her. I reached out to embrace her, and . . . .

I awoke suddenly, finding myself kicking the blanket off. The sun had already risen, but it hadn't been up long. Only a few embers remained of our campfire. I looked over to check on Lorena, but she wasn't there. I looked to the horses. They were both standing at the water's edge where we had tied them. I got up and looked around to find her standing waist-deep, naked in the stream with her arms around her chest. I turned around, feeling ashamed that I caught her bathing.

"It's okay," she explained with a shiver in her voice. "You didn't see anything. Not that I wouldn't let you. I was hoping to take a bath before you woke up, but the water is much too cold."

I heard her step out of the water, but I remained still.

"All right, I'm covered."

"Can I trust you?" I asked with a laugh.

"No, but you can't stand there staring at the trees forever."

I turned around, and she was indeed covered. She had used her blanket to wrap around herself. I picked up each of the other blankets, and with one quick shake, they disappeared, returning to the magical realm from which I made them.

Holding her arms up, Lorena said, "You can take this one, if you want."

I declined with a shake of my head and turned away again when I saw her begin to remove it to, hopefully, put some clothes on.

"Come on. It'll be fun. This has been a long trip already, and we're out here in the woods alone."

She ran her fingers through my hair and rubbed my ears. I quickly turned to face her. "I said—"

Before I could finish, Lorena pulled me close and kissed me. Her tongue reached past my lips, and I felt a bare leg slide up the back of mine before she pulled away, biting my lip in the process. I blinked to regain my balance and took a breath of air after she had taken it away.

"Well?" she asked with her hands on her naked hips.

I was speechless. I stood there for a moment longer before turning away to stamp out the last remnants of the campfire.

"You're dead!" she yelled at me, throwing her white blanket, hitting me in the back of the head.

I shook it away like the others and untied the horses.

Lorena quickly dressed, got on her horse, and rode off ahead of me, splashing through the water to follow the road that continued on the other side of the stream. Mariana and I hurried to catch up, and she finally slowed, so we could travel together.

With a sigh, I began to apologize. "Lorena, I'm sorry. I can't deny that I didn't like it…"

"Of course you liked it; I'm gorgeous," she interrupted.

"Yes, you are a gorgeous woman, but my heart still aches for Jinxie," I continued explaining. "Not only do I feel I would be cheating on her, I'm not in love with you."

Without looking at me, she argued, "Who said anything about love? I just wanted to roll around in the leaves with you."

"I'm sorry, but I follow my heart. Either my heart's in it fully or it's not at all."

"Ugh," she grunted her disapproval. "You're so black and white."

Rubbing my head and looking at my pale arms, I responded smartly, "Well, yeah, I am."

"Leave your heart out of this!"

"Hmm, I wonder if I could do that," I began to

think aloud. "I'm sure it would be messy; I'd have to break the ribcage. To keep the rest of my organs from failing, I would have to keep my blood circulating by magic. You may have to help me put it back in, though, or I'll be permanently undead."

Shaking her head, she asked harshly, "What are you jabbering about?"

"You said I should leave my heart out. I was just thinking how I could do it."

Stopping her horse, "I did say that, but I didn't mean literally! I didn't mean for you to kill yourself!"

"Kill myself? That's ridiculous," I argued, slapping lazily at her. "I think I know enough about the body to keep myself running. And perhaps I would prefer to be undead."

"Ambros, you scare me." She then rode on.

"No, just think for a moment," I told her, catching up to ride side by side. "Pain and suffering reminds us that we're mortal. If we're balanced between life and death, we wouldn't be affected by either."

"But how would we ever reach Valhalla to see those who died before us?"

"What if there is no Valhalla?"

"What if there is no Sun?"

I didn't answer. I merely looked up to it, squinting under its light.

"You know what I mean," she began correcting herself. "No Sun where the dead go to spend eternity. And what kind of existence is that, anyway? You sit around and talk to your friends and family—forever. Talk about boring," she expressed, rolling her eyes. "I'd much rather spend eternity in Valhalla where you go to battle with your friends and family because it's fun. I mean, it's not like you can die again, right? And you can eat and drink all day, and your ass never gets fat."

I laughed. "You make it sound like such a great place. Have you been there?"

This time it was she who slapped a hand at me. "No, silly. You have to die to get there. People just talk about it."

"Did any of those people die and come back?"

She began to answer but went quiet.

Looking around at the reds and yellows of the fall leaves and the pretty blue sky, I asked her, "Wouldn't it be nice if we could create our own world just for the people we care about?"

"It would be nice, but I still think Valhalla would be the perfect place for me. I'm sure my girl, Piper, is there waiting for me."

CHAPTER VII

THE GUARDIAN OF ASHWOOD

While we sat by the fire, I finally asked why she lied about how she acquired her ship.

She stood up and walked around the campfire. "I was hoping you didn't hear that," she began, referring to what Maddox said before trying to kill her. "If I told you the truth, I didn't think you would trust me."

"I trust you even less because you lied," I explained.

She laughed. "I'm a pirate," she announced with a bow. "It's in my nature to lie, cheat, and steal."

"But why?"

"Because being good is boring," she answered bluntly, raising her hands to the dark sky. "If you don't trust me, why didn't you leave on your own once we docked?"

"Because we have a deal; I owe you a sword."

Shaking her finger at me, she said, "Ah, you're a man of your word. You'll get nowhere in life that way." She came to sit next to me and leaned her head against my shoulder. "But I'm glad you are."

"So you stole that ship from Maddox?"

She lifted her head and began to explain. "Yes, but there's more to it than that. Maddox was a crewman on the Crimson Spear when my father captained the ship. He and a handful of others returned to the restaurant late one evening with news that my father and most of the crew had been killed, claiming they were the lucky few who escaped. My father had made many enemies in his day, but Maddox's story seemed a bit too vague for me to believe, especially with him now captaining the ship. Instead of calling him a liar outright, I volunteered to come aboard with the women who would cook and entertain the men. While at sea, I showed interest in Maddox, so he would lower his guard. When we reached port, I did some investigating. I found out that Maddox and the other men who claimed they narrowly escaped death had been paid a small fortune to betray my father and their crewmates. I informed the women of their deception, and they helped me take back my father's ship."

Enthralled by the story, I asked, "What did you do?"

Lorena got up to stoke the fire. "While we wined and dined at a restaurant in the city where we had docked for the evening, I had some of the women lead the trusted crewmen back to the ship. The remaining women and I seduced the men and rented rooms for the evening where we tied them to the beds. We set the place afire and returned to the ship. I believed him to be dead, but he…"

I held a hand up to quiet her, and I looked at Mariana who was standing nearby. We heard leaves being trampled in the distance.

"It sounds like horses!" Lorena said, frightened by whatever was quickly approaching.

We stood together with our backs to the fire and our swords at the ready. Mariana raised a hand to point into the darkness, but she was knocked aside by four large creatures as they burst out of the forest! They had a long body with four legs and the head and arms similar to that of a hairy man. The hair covering their bodies was short and bristly, but they had a long mane and tail like a horse. Two of the creatures drew bows and held us in their sites while the other two circled the camp.

More amazed than she was frightened, Lorena whispered, "Centaurs! I've heard tales of them from travelers. Lower your swords."

I didn't argue. If the centaurs wanted to kill us, they would have already fired their arrows. I sheathed my swords, and we held our hands up.

One stamped out our fire. Another kicked Ralph, causing him to collapse into a heap of bones. It then removed the pack on Lorena's horse and freed it.

"Oh, come on! We need those," I pleaded.

One of the large beasts galloped up to me, speaking in a strange, animal language composed of brays, blows, and snorts while he stamped his front hooves.

"You don't happen to know their language, too, do you?" I asked Lorena without looking away from the seven feet tall creature.

"Call it a hunch, but I don't think they like us

setting fire in the forest or enslaving horses."

The beast moved in close, but I didn't back away. It snorted, and the four creatures disappeared into the forest.

"Great," I announced dryly, peering off in the direction Lorena's horse ran. "It looks like Ralph will have to bear us both." Laughing, I added, "He won't be happy."

"But they broke him," Lorena said, pointing at his remains before watching me resurrect him again. She then ran to check on Mariana. "Oh no!"

Upon inspecting her for myself, I saw that many of her bones were crushed. "She has sustained too much damage," I informed Lorena. "She wouldn't be much use to us if I were to bring her back."

"What are we going to do about a night watch-men?"

"I'll stay up."

She opened her mouth to object, but I assured her it would be okay and that humans needed more sleep than elves, anyway.

We located our satchels where the centaur dropped them and rested at the foot of a tree. Without a warm fire to sleep by, Lorena slept huddled up next to me. I remained awake, listening to the wind and her snoring.

Lorena awoke before dawn, so we rode on to Ashwood, arriving just after noon. Too faint for human ears, I heard, "Ambros returns! Ambros returns!"

Lorena stayed closer to me upon seeing Dark Elves step out of the shadows of trees. Unlike me, who learned to weave clothing from magic during my time with the Light Elves, my Dark Elf kin wore the furs of animals and pieces of tree bark to aid them in blending with the forest. By the time we reached the obsidian doors, many elves were already there to welcome me.

The doors opened, and Torvin stepped out to see me again after a century and a half. I gasped at the sight of him. His right hand was completely gone. His arm had healed over at the wrist where his hand should've been. He also had a terrible scar running from his left eye down his face. The eye was still in its socket but milky white.

I was in disbelief at the horrible wounds he had suffered. "Torvin, old friend, what happened?"

"Who is this human you've brought with you?" Torvin asked suspiciously, ignoring my question.

"This is Captain Lorena," I answered, and she removed her hat to take a bow. "I was on my way here from the Council Palace when I was struck down. Lorena was kind enough to help me on my journey."

"Welcome, Captain," he said before turning back to me. Placing a hand on my shoulder, he said, "Come with me. I fear Ashwood is in great danger, my friend."

Leaving Ralph outside, we followed Torvin, but he led us into a side tunnel to speak to me in private. "I wish I had better news for you, but if your father foresaw what would happen after his departure, he didn't warn any of us."

"Why? What's happened?"

Torvin was a master swordsman and hunter. He had been training our people since before I was born. I had never known him to fear anything, but I could hear in his voice now that he was afraid, and that terrified me.

He took a moment to see who may be within listening distance before he filled me in on the details. "Your father was a great leader, Ambros, and we all miss him dearly, more now than ever. He served on the Council of Dragons for centuries, quietly protecting us from their devious talons. We were under the impression that Magnus would do the same in Ambrosius' absence, but Magnus didn't stay to protect us from the dragon menace that continues to grow in the east. He left to pursue his own crusade, leaving a child vampire among us. I caught the girl feeding on Takarha while, at the same time, giving her blood. When I intervened, she attacked me. I was caught off guard by her speed and magical aptitude. I lost my hand, and my eye was damaged before I could restrain her."

"What happened to her?" I asked anxiously. "Where is she, now?"

"Takarha died from blood loss," he answered sadly. "Without Magnus here to determine a proper punishment, I took the vampire to the Council Palace myself. It was there I found Grimlash the Hydra Lord had already captured and was interrogating Magnus, the one called Dirk, and a necromancer I did not know. There was nothing I could do for them. Before leaving the palace to come home, I was informed that Grimlash destroyed the vampire."

"Oh, Eve," I exhaled, looking down as tears threatened to break, remembering my first real friend. I felt Lorena's hand close over mine to console me.

"I'm sorry," Torvin apologized.

"I don't blame you," I told him, wiping my eyes. "You did what you must for the city."

Torvin shook his head. "But that was just the beginning of our problems. It wasn't long before the council sent a real dragon to rule over us. She informed us that Grimlash had perished and Elsbareth the White had taken over as head of the World Council. She took up residence at your home and has continued the experiments your father logged in his notes."

"Oh no!"

"What? What kind of experiments?" Lorena asked.

"I need to get over there. I need to see what she's done," I said, beginning to leave the tunnel we had been quietly talking in.

Torvin grabbed my shoulder to stop me. "I must warn you: Yndra is very powerful. She has a deceptive tongue. Don't let her words twist your beliefs."

I nodded that I understood before leading Lorena through the illuminated tunnels to Ashwood. The sun was still shining through the obsidian roof, casting an otherworldly blue light over the city. Standing atop the stone steps, I breathed deeply the earthy rich air and smiled, forgetting for a moment the gravity of the situation. I remembered gathering animals from my traps in the forest and walking down these ancient stone steps to carry them home to experiment on. While the other children learned to fashion obsidian into arrowheads and jewelry, I was preoccupied with learning the anatomy of different animals. If all creatures go to the sun after they die, I wondered if they could be brought back just the way they were. I still wondered.

Lorena was in awe of the view. "In all my years of travel, I have never seen such beauty." She then quickly turned and kissed my lips, catching me by surprise.

"You little sneak," I laughed.

"I suppose you could say I pirated that kiss." She smacked my butt and skipped down the stairs. "Now let's go meet this Yndra; I'm dying to see my first dragon."

"And you just might," I warned.

She waited at the bottom of the stairs for me to catch up. She then wrapped her arm around mine, and we walked through the city. Ashwood looked the same as I remembered it. Houses were built around trees. Mushrooms and molds grew along the forest floor and even on homes. I don't believe a human could live in those conditions for very long before getting sick.

I noticed a leather satchel she had slung over her shoulder, hanging down between us. Curious, I asked, "What do you carry in your bag?"

Politely, she answered, "Oh, a woman never knows when she may need a brush, hair ribbons, or perhaps a vial of poison."

"HA! Sounds like you came prepared."

Batting her lashes at me, she responded, "I'm always prepared."

Elves sat outside their homes smoking pipes after a hard night's work in the mines. They nodded to us as we passed. Fairies flew down from their lofty, treetop dwellings to welcome me back with their sweet voices and ask who my lovely friend was.

"I can't get over how simply wondrous this place is," Lorena commented.

"Then you should see Lylandria, the city of the Light Elves. If you worship the Sun, that's the place to live."

"I thought the Dark Elves worshiped the Sun, too. Why do they live down here in this cavern?"

"They do. As far as I know, all elves worship the Sun. The Dark Elves live down here because they fear the rest of the world. They want no part of the wars and conflicts of other races."

"Fear?" Lorena repeated. "But there's so much to learn from all life," she argued.

"I know that, but the rest of my kin don't care. They don't care what happens outside their hunting grounds that surround the city."

Upon reaching the place I once lived, there was nothing left of it to remember. Both the tree and the house were gone! In its place was a tower built of black obsidian as wide as the surrounding homes and as tall as the trees.

"Was this where you lived?" Lorena asked, looking up at the dark tower.

"This is the place but not the house."

"Well, this house is amazing!"

"Pfft! Come on," I told her, stepping up to the door to enter.

Inside, the first floor of the tower was one big room. There were three tables with books and scrolls scattered about them. To our left was a staircase leading down, and to our right, stairs leading up. Above us, there was a large, green obsidian egg protruding from the middle of the floor above us. The silhouette of a dark, serpentine shape could be seen within the glowing egg.

"What is that?" Lorena asked me.

Before I could answer, a voice interrupted. "Magnificent, isn't she?"

We turned to see a devilish woman coming

down the stairs to meet us. She wore a sultry red dress with a bleached bone belt and matching necklace. She was as curvaceous as Lorena but had soft black skin, a crown of black horns, and a sharp tail.

"Ambros, I am overjoyed to see you've come home," she said to me with a bow. Her voice was smooth and soulful. "And who is this beautiful woman that you've brought with you?"

Lorena removed her hat and bowed graciously. "I am Captain Eleanor Lorena of the Crimson Spear and owner of the Legs & Tail: Lobster Barrel Buffet and Brothel, the hottest restaurant on the Mediterranean."

"Eleanor?" I repeated, thinking Lorena was her only name.

"Oh, I love her," the strange woman said to me before hugging Lorena. Looking her over, the dark woman said, "I could just eat you up."

"Believe me, I'd let you," Lorena teased the woman with a wink.

"Where are my manners," another voice with the same soulful tone said from behind us, and an identical woman wearing an identical red dress came from downstairs. "My name is Yndra the Black," she announced with a bow. She then removed a dark gauntlet from her hand and placed it on the table.

Looking from one to the other, Lorena announced, excitedly, "Twins! I like where this is going."

I shook my head and rolled my eyes at her comment. "Which one of you were the first?" I asked seriously, knowing what experiments Yndra had been conducting. "And are there anymore of you?"

The Yndra that just walked into the room from

downstairs raised her hand and smiled. "I am the first, and it's just the two of us for now."

"I suppose that will make me Yndra the Second," the woman that we met first announced.

Looking to the egg suspended above us, I asked, "And how long before Yndra the Third hatches?"

Leaning against the edge of a table, Yndra the First answered, "About a month."

"How many more do you plan to create?"

"However many more it takes," Yndra the Second answered.

Before I could ask the next logical question, Yndra the First stood from the table and motioned for us to follow her. I began following the two women upstairs before noticing that Lorena wasn't behind me. She was still looking around at things on the tables. "Would you feel better waiting outside?" I asked her, the three of us stopping on the stairs to look down at her.

"No, I'm coming," she said, adjusting her hat before following us upstairs to another laboratory where we could view the top half of the glowing obsidian egg.

I stepped up close to the egg and peered in to see the Black Dragon forming within the magical elixir. "So what body part did you use to copy yourself?"

"Oh, I used an eye just like your father. Dragons are blessed with regeneration," one of the Yndra's explained while they brought chairs over for us to sit in.

I turned away from the egg and noticed through the open windows of the tower that the daylight hours of Ashwood had already ended. This may be another long night, I thought to myself.

We were invited to sit near the obsidian egg which gave off a soothing warmth. I motioned for

Lorena to sit in the chair closest to the stairs leading down, and I sat next to her.

"Would you like a drink?" Yndra asked, filling a mug from a barrel she had at the end of a table.

"No, thank you," I answered. "I don't drink anything that a serpent poured."

"I would," Lorena raised her hand. "I'll drink his, too." She removed her hat and hung it over the corner of her chair.

I shook my head and struggled to contain my laughter. "Of course you would."

Both Yndra's laughed, and the one pouring the mugs brought two over for Lorena. "This is Ashwood Ale, the stoutest ale in the entire world."

Lorena wasted no time in taking a swallow. She turned her head to the side and blew. "Now that's good ale." She then sat one of the mugs on the table behind us and continued drinking.

The dark women poured themselves a mug and sat down. "Ambrosius was a brilliant sorcerer," one of them began. "I wish he were here, now; I could really use his help," she added sadly.

"Pop would never help you!" I fired at her.

The women laughed. "And yet, he has," one said, motioning to the other and to the obsidian egg.

"The great dragon clans were summoned by Grimlash," the other began. "They were asked to assemble at the newly constructed palace where he would lay out his plan to immediately eradicate a large percentage of the world's population. Magnus the Red Dragon Lord of Ashwood killed him but ultimately fell at the hands of Elsbareth the White. She took over as head of the council and relayed the terrible news to us when the clans arrived. The council's plan of conquest was delayed, and I was ordered to replace Magnus here. No one knew about the immense trove of knowledge left behind by your father…"

"You call him Pop," Lorena interrupted, clearly drunk as she reached the bottom of her second mug.

One of the women filled another mug, but when she brought it to Lorena, the drunken captain began to fall out of her chair. While still holding the mug, Yndra moved her tail around to stop Lorena from falling.

"I'm okay. I'm okay," Lorena said loudly. "I can drink more than two."

I slid my chair closer, and put my arm around her to hold her up.

"Oh, look at you," she said with glassy eyes. "Looking to get lucky with us girls tonight, are ya? We may let you watch." She leaned her head on my shoulder and went quiet.

I pushed the blonde tresses out of her face and wiped the dribble of ale from her lip. "It seems she finally found a drink that's stronger than her." I suddenly saw the flesh of her face wither and fall away, so I shut my eyes. I couldn't sit there while she appeared to decompose on me. I carefully stood up, so she could lay across my chair.

"You see it don't you?" Yndra asked excitedly. "It's in your eyes."

I looked at her, but both women looked as devilishly beautiful as before while Lorena appeared as a rotting corpse. Astonished, I asked, "How is it that you look alive?"

"A transmutation spell reconstructs the body to match the perfect vision one has of oneself, which conceals their true form to all those around them, even you," she explained.

"And how is it you know what I see?"

"Ambrosius wrote that he and all of his copies had the extrasensory perception which, according to his notes, is a glimpse of a mere fraction of the future."

I walked over to the obsidian egg with my arms crossed. "For as long as I can remember, I've seen people as if they were decomposing. It only lasts a moment, and sometimes I'll go a week or longer without it happening."

"You're seeing their mortality, their eventual death."

I looked back at Lorena, but the vision had already passed. She looked as beautiful as she always did. "But I never see myself this way. Why?"

Both women were fixed in the same pose as they thought. They sat with legs crossed, touching their chin before one finally spoke. "Perhaps this view only works on others and not yourself."

"Or perhaps you will live forever," the other suggested with raised eyebrows.

"Ha! If pop couldn't live forever, certainly I wouldn't." Then I remembered what I was talking to and that I shouldn't become too comfortable around her. "Who have you told of my pop's experiments? Who else is growing copies of themselves? Answer me, serpent!"

She remained calm as she answered. "No one else knows. I've kept all of this a secret."

Confused, I asked, "Why? Why wouldn't you report it to your council?"

"Your father . . . I mean, Pop," she quickly corrected herself, "was regarded by many as being a great leader. He helped maintain balance in the world during a time when the dragons faced extinction. Peace is a rare quality among dragons. And after spending years deciphering and organizing his notes, I understand why. He was not a dragon at all."

The other dark woman stood from her chair to stand next to me by the obsidian egg. "I have a theory that your pop created the legendary dragon known as Shadowrath."

"Preposterous!" I spat.

Still looking down into the egg at the Black Dragon growing within, she said, "Think about it. There had never been another like him before his arrival nor after his demise."

"Why would Pop create such a terrible beast?" I asked, refusing to believe what I was hearing.

"The phoenixes, who we believe brought life to this planet, left to seed other worlds, leaving only one, Arethil. She remained to help life flourish. Even when dragons came to the surface, Arethil only wanted peace between the many races that inhabited this world. To the warmongering dragons, peace was not an option, and the surface dwellers were caught up in the battle for supremacy." Yndra turned to face me. "I believe Ambrosius created a monster that even the dragons feared, not to destroy what the phoenixes worked so hard to create, but to bring balance to it."

I stared into her black and red reptilian eyes as her words brought clarity to my father's past.

"It had become clear to your pop that the dragons would devastate the earth. Something drastic needed to be done before all was lost, and so he created the most terrible serpent this world has ever seen and released it upon the world to reduce the dragon population."

The other Yndra walked over and placed a hand on my shoulder. "Ambros, without your pop here to help us, we now look to you."

Concerned by what I believed her to be saying, I asked, "You don't mean to bring Shadowrath back into this world? I will not!"

"No," she answered. "I mean to kill my kind."

"What?" My thoughts came to a screeching halt. "Then why are you making copies of yourself?"

"Because I cannot do this alone," she answered sadly. "And I definitely cannot trust my kin," she added.

"I suppose not," I agreed with her.

"I believe in the work your father was doing. This world cannot sustain us all. You were created to continue his work, of that I'm sure. And I believe Magnus did exactly what he was meant to: remove Grimlash from power. Without his diabolical mind to lead them, the council was severely weakened. And three days ago, I received news that his successor, Elsbareth the White, had been killed and that Assim the Yellow has stepped up to lead."

"Did he kill her to take the throne?"

Shaking her head, she answered, "No. I was told that a plague spread among the elves and infected a dragon. While trying to kill them, Elsbareth was bitten. She began showing signs of the infection, so the other dragons present had no choice but to kill her."

That happened while I was there. Kronyx was the infected dragon who bit Elsbareth, I thought to myself.

Both women took hold of my hands, drawing me

from my thoughts. "We desperately need your help, Ambros."

Looking around, I told her, "It appears you have everything under control to me."

"The thing about dragons is we have exceptional hearing. I can hear everything that goes on in this city. I know Torvin told you about the child vampire that attacked him. What he didn't tell you is that Takarha rose from her death. Fearing she would be killed, she fled Ashwood. But news has reached my ears that a demon resides in a town not far to the east, and the people there are being transformed into demons! We can't let this get out of control."

"Why haven't you already paid this little town a visit?"

Shaking her head, "Foolishly, I paid it no mind until I heard what happened at the palace."

"What is it that you plan to do, now?"

"I know you have spent your life studying the undead. I would like you to destroy the infected, so it spreads no further and bring Takarha here, unhurt. Bring her home."

I laughed. "And what do think you can do for her?"

With a confident smile, she answered, "I believe that you and I together can cure her."

I said nothing while I thought of what I could learn from this endeavor. Unlike a zombie, who loses connection to its memories because their blood no longer flows, a vampire's blood keeps the mind active and heals the body of even the gravest wounds. They both are considered undead, trapped between life and death, but a vampire is closer to the living than they are to the dead. If it is possible to bring Jinxie back to life, perhaps curing Takarha of vampirism will lead me in the right direction. I looked at Yndra and nodded that I will try to bring Takarha back.

"Excellent. The sooner you get started, the better."

I started to wake Lorena when I turned back to the two women. "Before I go, there's something you may be able to help me with." I pulled the pouch of ashes from my belt and handed it to them. "This is all I have left of Jinxie of Lylandria, my mate."

An expression of sincere sadness befell the two women, and one carefully took the pouch from me with both hands. She took a pinch of the ashes to examine closer. "To bring one back from ashes would be quite a feat indeed, but I will do some experiments while you're gone. Perhaps I will know if it can be done before you return."

"Thank you."

I looked at Lorena who was still sleeping across the chairs.

"She'll be all right here. Don't worry about her."

"That's just it," I told her while gently rubbing Lorena's cheek. "I will worry about her. At least, if she's with me, I can keep an eye on her."

Lorena's eyes opened halfway. "Why, hello handsome," she said groggily. "Did I miss anything exciting?"

I clearly liked being called handsome. "Come on, Captain. It's time to go. Do you feel up to walking?"

I helped her stand, but she felt no ill effects from the ale she drank earlier. She straightened her shirt before pulling a brush from her satchel to fix her hair.

"Be careful," both of the dragon ladies told us before we left.

Downstairs, Lorena put her hat on, and we stepped out of the tower. "So, where are we headed?" she asked, wrapping her arm around mine.

"Well, I thought we'd head over to see the Master Enchanter, so you can choose a weapon."

She squealed with excitement and squeezed me tightly, causing me to laugh.

As we walked through the dimly-lit city, I told her about the Draconian Wars that drove my people here and how we began mining volcanic glass to make weapons.

"But the wars are over. Why doesn't your people explore the world and build new cities?" she asked.

"When every couple has only two children, the population of their people never grows," I explained. "The Dark Elves fight to hold onto the surrounding forests, but they don't try to expand their borders; they have all the land they need to sustain themselves."

"Perhaps one day I will settle down with a good man . . . or three," she added with raised eyebrows, "live on a nice, secluded island, and have five or six children."

"Five or six!"

"But not today," she laughed.

At the edge of the city, carved from the very wall of the dormant volcano, were three temples. A large vein of blue obsidian ran down from above the center temple and divided around it to look like a frozen waterfall. The Dark Elves' Master Enchanter, Desynger, lived in the temple on the right. A colorful, stone walkway led upstairs between tall columns. We stopped for a moment, so she could marvel at the black stone dwelling.

"Wow!" Lorena whispered.

"These were the first homes built when my people arrived eons ago."

We stepped inside to a long room with many stone tables and wooden chairs. Obsidian weapons of all makes and colors decorated the walls. I followed Lorena around the room to admire the many swords, daggers, spears, staves, axes, and even bows and arrows.

Taking a red sword with a finely carved bone handle from its hanger, she said, "Hold out your arm; I want to see what it does."

"HA! You're crazy!" I told her. "Even if it has no enchantment, it will still sever my arm!"

She laughed and began swinging the sword around her wildly, pretending she didn't know how to wield it. "I know what it does! I know what it does!" she announced, laughing hysterically. "It makes you crazy!"

"You were already crazy before you picked it up," I chuckled, backing away from her.

"Ambros, is that you?" a familiar voice asked from behind me, and Lorena stopped swinging the sword. "I didn't think I would see you again."

I turned to see Desynger standing in the room, and I bowed to him.

"By Arethil's fire! You look just like him." With a glimmer of happiness in his eyes, he made his way over to us with the help of a cane and placed a feeble hand on my shoulder. Looking me over, he said, "You look exactly like Ambrosius when I took his class on enchanting bones."

"I didn't know he taught a class."

"Oh yes, he taught for many years before creating you," he said, pulling a chair out to sit in. The old master wore animal furs like the other elves of Ashwood, but he also wore a strange belt that looked like a chain with obsidian stones set into it. I imagined each stone was enchanted with a different power.

"You're right," he answered suddenly with a grin. Pointing to a blue stone on the belt, he said, "This one allows me to read the thoughts of those around me."

"You probably shouldn't read her thoughts," I warned with a laugh, pointing at Lorena.

"And why not?" she asked, already knowing what I was getting at. "There's nothing wrong with my thoughts."

Desynger chuckled and told us, "I already know them. You're curious what that sword in your hands can do. Well, it causes blood to violently explode. The more blood it comes into contact with, the bigger the explosions."

Both Lorena and I cringed at the thought before she announced, "I WANT IT!"

Desynger and I both laughed at her excitement, and I told her, "If that's the one you want, it's yours unless Master Desynger says no."

She looked at him, and he gave a simple nod that she could have the slender, red obsidian sword.

"YES! Thank you! Thank you! Thank you!" she said to the old Dark Elf, quickly sheathing the sword and strapping it to her belt.

I sat down to listen to the aging master while Lorena continued looking around the room.

Touching the stones on his belt, Desynger said to me, "Ambrosius never liked using enchanted items to gain power. He preferred having the power himself, but he never did figure out how to create life without using the egg. When I was a young boy, my father told me that Ambrosius created himself a new body before his wore out. I didn't understand why anyone would want to continue living life over and over until I myself grew old and feeble. I don't want to die," he confessed. "I'd rather be your age again, gallivantin' around with some buxom blonde." He then pointed to the captain who was still admiring the many weapons that hung around the room.

I burst into laughter, shocked by what I just heard the Master Enchanter say.

Lorena spun around and pointed to me. "See? You should listen to your elders. You should enjoy what you have while you have it."

"Even at 970 years old, I feel my life was a mere flash of sunlight in the darkness of this dreadful cave."

"So you don't look forward to going to the Sun?"

"What good am I to our people there?" he questioned. "From childhood, we're fed the story of the great phoenixes and the kingdom of the Sun where we'll all go some day. By not fearing death, we fail to conquer life's greatest adversary. Now, I have too few sunrises left to make a difference."

Remembering my mission, I stood up quickly. "Oh, speaking of sunrise, we have to get going!"

"You young people are always in a hurry." Desynger positioned his cane and began to stand. Lorena stepped over to help him. "Thank you, my dear." Looking back at me, he said, "Just make sure you use your time wisely, young one."

The old elf saw us to the door and followed us out to the stone steps. "You know, Ambrosius attempted to transport himself though time, but he found that the very process of traveling creates an alternate universe."

"Say that again," I asked of him, unsure if I heard correctly.

"Look at it from another perspective. Let's say you decide that you would rather not exist at all, so you go back in time and smash your egg while baby Ambros is still developing inside. Do you see what I'm getting at?"

With that analogy, it became clear. "Pop couldn't accomplish his goal by jumping through time."

Snapping his fingers, he pointed at me, signaling that I was correct. "You got it. And without an anchor to this world, you may never find your way home. I lost my son to the gateway of time."

"Stenwick is gone? I'm sorry to hear that. He was a good elf. We were never close growing up, but then again, I was never really close to anyone here. What happened?"

"He believed he could convince the ancient elves to stand together against the Dragon race instead of being tempted by them to separate during the Great Winter."

"Was that my father's plan?"

Shrugging his shoulders, Desynger answered, "I don't know. Much like you, he remained distant."

"And what am I supposed to do?"

He shook his head. "I don't know that either."

I pointed at his belt. "Don't you have some sort of a stone that can help?"

"On life's great journey, we must all make our

own path."

I nodded and told him goodbye. Lorena kissed his cheek and thanked him again for the sword. As we walked across the colorful obsidian stones to leave, Master Desynger said loudly to me, "I know you lack faith in yourself, but I still have faith in you, young Ambrosius. You will fulfill your father's plan, whatever it may be, I am sure of this."

CHAPTER VIII

VAMPIRE HUNTER

Moonlight illuminated the forest outside the city of Ashwood. I placed a hand against the obsidian doors and they closed. I called for Torvin who was with other elves nearby skinning rabbits. I requested a horse for Lorena to ride back to the coast and food for the journey.

"But I want to go with you," she pleaded as Torvin left to fetch a horse.

Shaking my head, I told her, "Where I'm going may be a bit too dangerous."

"Then it's too dangerous for you to go alone," she argued.

Torvin led a horse over and another elf brought a satchel with supplies and a skin of water.

Looking at the horse and back to me with sadness in her eyes, she said, "This is goodbye then."

I nodded slowly. "Thank you for—"

She suddenly grabbed me, pulling me in for a kiss, and again, her tongue reached in to taste me. I didn't pull away from her, and I didn't remain still this time. I held her and tasted her mouth. Secretly, I had hoped she would kiss me again. She may not have my heart, but I will miss her.

Without another word, she climbed on her horse and road off into the darkness.

Whispering, I said, "Goodbye, Captain Eleanor Lorena." I stood there until I could no longer hear her before summoning my horse, Ralph, which had collapsed into a heap of bones not far from the entrance to the city. Making sure Scourge and Devour were secured on my back, I created a thick blanket over the boney spine of the horse. I mounted up and headed east to find Takarha.

The town wasn't far. I reached it well before sunrise, so I had time to locate the vampire during her usual feeding time.

I found it strange that there were no torches lit. There was no candlelight coming from any of the windows as I rode into town. I then noticed that every home and building was in disarray. Doors were missing, windows were broken, and roofs were rotting away.

The night air blew cold, and snow began to fall. I stopped my skeletal horse and rubbed my hands together, magically forming gloves over them to help them stay warm. I began rubbing my arms and concentrating on the clothes I was wearing, causing them to thicken with fur. I pulled at my collar, and the material began to form a fur lined hood to cover my head.

I continued on slowly through the desolate town

while snow fell in thick, fluffy flakes. Near the opposite end of town, there was a large building with doors still attached and a roof that looked to be still intact. I decided to go inside to have a look around and get out of the snow. I stepped off my horse and walked to the building with my arms tight around me. The latch was broken, so I pushed the creaky door open and stepped inside. Even among the broken furniture and cobwebs, I could tell the place was once a nice bar.

The night vision elves are blessed with helped me navigate the various debris that littered the floor while I made my way to the fireplace. I stacked a couple pieces of rotten firewood and broken chair legs. Removing a glove for a moment, I held my hand over the wood and focused my energy to ignite it.

After taking a moment to warm my cold bones by the fire, I felt ready to look around. Next to the fireplace was a doorway into an adjoining house. There was a bedchamber straight ahead and a hallway to my left that led to a back room. Behind the bar, I noticed a door leading to another room. Inside, the wooden planks of the floor had been broken up to reveal a storage room beneath the building. Through the darkness below, I saw many stacked barrels. I climbed down to the dirt floor. The barrels were heavy, most likely full of mead.

The walls were dirt with wooden beams and boards used to help strengthen them under the weight of the house above. Leading away from the house, I found a small tunnel behind a stack of barrels. I bent down and looked in, speculating it led to the basement of the house next door.

"What if it collapses on me?" I whispered to myself. "What if Takarha is at the other end?"

I listened for a moment, hearing nothing but my own heartbeat. I sniffed the air, catching only a dull, earthy smell. I closed my eyes and dug my fingers into the dirt. I could feel that I was close.

I was apprehensive about entering the long tunnel, but I needed to see where exactly it led. I looked around once more before crawling in on my hands and knees. My night vision cut through the darkness, allowing me to see that it was clear ahead and there were no traps within the narrow passage.

It took a few minutes for me to crawl through to the other end. When I stood up and dusted myself off, I saw that the basement was not filled with barrels of mead but with long crates. I counted more than two dozen in the room. I stepped over to the nearest one and carefully slid the lid over far enough to peek inside.

"Dirt?"

I checked the next crate to find that it, too, was filled with dirt. I reached in to scoop up a bit when a hand suddenly burst from it, grabbing my wrist!

"SHIT!"

The lids of all the crates flew open and people began climbing out of the dirt that filled them.

I tried pulling myself away from the hand that held me as my captor rose from the soft dirt covering him. I unsheathed a sword with my free hand and hacked at his wrist. Severing his hand, I pulled away. I quickly sheathed my sword and leaped back into the tunnel, scrambling through without fear of it collapsing but of being caught by the undead humans that were now funneling in behind me!

"Come on, guys, you don't want me," I yelped while scurrying through the tunnel. "I'm just a scrawny, little elf boy. I barely have enough blood for me. I surely don't have enough for all of you."

Once I escaped, I pushed a stack of barrels over to barricade the tunnel. A couple of them exploded on impact, spilling their contents. I climbed out of the basement and ran back into the bar. Still sensing the undead approaching, I drew Devour which I always sheathe over my right shoulder. A swirling mist of energy could be seen within the enchanted obsidian blade. Through the broken windows, I could see Ralph waiting where I left him in the deepening snow.

A creak of the wooden floor alerted me of something behind me. I turned to see the silhouette of someone standing in the doorway to the adjoining house, and they leaped across the room toward me! I moved aside, swinging my sword, but tripped over a heap of broken furniture. I quickly climbed to my feet and saw that it was a human woman that attacked me. Baring sharp fangs, she hissed at me. Her skin was dirty and pale, much like the people downstairs. Her hair was a tangled mess, and she wore ruined clothes.

"Where is Takarha?" I asked.

The vampire circled me slowly, careful not to find herself on the end of my sword.

Focusing my thoughts onto her, I asked again, "Where is Takarha?"

The woman cackled. "You have no power over me, elf."

I mocked her cackling laughter, angering her.

A wild-eyed, stocky man ran into the room. "Ah, let's bleed him before the others get here."

"You don't want my blood; it's way too salty."

I eased my way back to the door with my sword

held between me and the two vampires. I stepped out into the blowing snow. With unwavering stares, the two vampires followed me.

I caught movement from the corner of my left eye of someone stepping out of a house. While still facing the two following me, I noticed the person run out into the street toward me. I waited until the last possible second before swinging my sword. They fell hard into the snow, their head rolling away from their body.

"You have no head. What do you think about that?"

I sent a mental command to Ralph to charge the vampires, and he immediately responded. The woman was knocked down, but the man attacked me. I stepped out of reach of his nasty claws. I raised my sword, severing his hand. The man screamed out while his arm began deteriorating, but he continued his attacks. I took another step back before lunging forward to push the enchanted sword into his chest. He fought against the curse that burned through his veins to no avail. While struggling to reach me, his body began crumbling away until he collapsed into the snow.

Tears of blood streamed down the woman's face as she screamed.

"Well, it seems I have power over you after all," I taunted. Her eyes shifted to look past me for a brief moment, and I turned to see the town's people coming out of the dilapidated homes. They were all pale and wearing ragged clothing.

I began laughing at the overwhelming odds against me. "Now, it's getting interesting."

Reaching out to the two dead vampires, I called

to their bones to rise up and aid me in battle.

"Leave my husband alone!" the woman ordered, charging in to attack. She clawed my face in the blink of an eye, leaving four nasty cuts from my mouth to my right ear. She screamed at me, and I saw her face begin to shrivel. It was then that I noticed she had impaled herself onto my sword. Her cries waned, and she slid from the blade.

The two skeletons that I had summoned broke free of their withered flesh like butterflies from a cocoon, and I sent them into battle against the approaching vampires. Ralph kicked and trampled my adversaries while the two skeletons grappled with them.

I drew Scourge from its sheath and fought off all who attacked me. Those wounded by it saw everyone as a threat, so they turned against their vampire brethren for a short while. Those cut by Devour felt their cold blood turn to ash, making their bodies unresponsive to their dark commands.

Over the sounds of undead attempting to reach me, I heard screams and wet explosions. As the sounds drew nearer, I saw Captain Lorena riding into the surrounding horde, swinging her enchanted sword. Whenever she struck one of the attacking vampires with the red obsidian sword, the force behind it sent an explosion ripping through their blood. She kissed at me and asked, "Miss me?"

"Actually, I did," I answered, holding my ground.

With her sword in one hand, she raised her other to reveal the gauntlet that Yndra wore back in Ashwood. Facing the palm of the powerful relic toward the vampires caused them to instantly burst into flames.

"How did you get that?" I asked, dislodging Scourge from the chest of a vampire. It hunched over and clenched its wound before turning against its undead brethren.

"I pirated it," she laughed, scorching all those around her.

The gauntlet emitted waves of intense heat from the blue obsidian gem set in its palm. It burned everything it was directed at, even melting through snow and igniting whatever sticks and leaves that lay beneath.

Lorena incinerated dozens before the gauntlet quit working, and the monsters dragged her from her horse. She was able to defend herself, but her horse could not. While they fought each other for its blood, Lorena scrambled over to me.

Shaking her gloved hand, she asked, "What happened to it?"

"It absorbs energy, so you must have expended all that it had stored."

"Great! Just great!"

While Lorena and I stood back to back, we were completely surrounded by the vampire horde, and I began to laugh.

"Why are you laughing?" I heard Lorena's trembling voice ask from behind me.

But I couldn't stop to answer. Stressful situations often caused me to laugh hysterically. The vampires clawed at us and gnashed their teeth, but were careful to stay just out of our reach.

"A Dark Elf!" I heard a child's voice say over the crowd. "Everyone stop!" she commanded. Silence fell over the town and everyone turned to the child standing on the roof of one of the houses. "This is one of my own."

While everyone was calm for a moment, I whistled for Ralph and the skeletons I had summoned to return.

"What's happening?" Lorena whispered to me. "Don't tell me these monsters are led by a little girl."

"Okay, I won't tell you."

The girl dropped down from the roof. The town's people, who had all been turned into vampires, divided for the girl to meet me. Once I saw who she was, I sheathed my swords.

"Takarha?" I asked, realizing that her body had been locked as a child since Eve made her a vampire a century and a half ago. Her lustrous black hair was worn long and straight just as I remembered it, but her skin seemed paler, almost translucent.

She broke into tears and wrapped her arms around me. "Ambros," she cried. "I'm sorry I was so mean to you."

"It's okay," I told her, remembering she avoided me for months after I wrote her a poem. "Those days have passed, but right now, we need you to come home."

Takarha stepped away from me. "I will not go back," she announced sternly. "This is my home, now. These are my people," she motioned to the surrounding undead humans. "We've tunneled beneath the city to hide from—"

The roar of a dragon caused everyone to instinctively duck their head, and darkness blotted out the starlight. A pungent, green liquid sprayed across many of the vampires, causing them to melt, bone and all.

"NO!" Takarha yelled up at the sky. "She's come for us!"

Taking hold of Takarha's hand, Lorena and I rushed her toward one of the old homes just as a huge Black Dragon splashed down onto the carnage and roared. It sprayed more of the liquefying toxin over vampires as they fled and swatted its tail to knock others into the bubbling pools.

Through the missing door of the house, I saw the dragon shrink in size to take a form I was more familiar with. Yndra walked through her toxin to the house. Lorena and I stood between her and Takarha with our swords drawn.

Yndra bowed to me. "Thank you both for luring her and her undead progeny out into the open. Blood will do that, but not my blood. The scent of dragon blood only frightens them deeper into their burrows."

"She doesn't want to go back," I told her.

With a smile, she responded, "It is not her decision to make, nor is it yours."

Yndra spun around, whipping me and Lorena away with her long, black tail. She grabbed Takarha by the wrist and began dragging her out of the house.

"No! NO!" she screamed, struggling to pull herself free.

Yndra picked her up and leaped into the air where she transformed back into a dragon and carried Takarha to Ashwood.

I sheathed my swords and helped Lorena to her feet. "Come on! Something bad is about to happen!"

Running outside, she stepped over a partially liquefied arm. "What's about to happen?"

I whistled for Ralph, and he galloped up from between the houses where he had dodged Yndra's attacks. Lorena and I climbed on and headed back to Ashwood as quickly as he could carry us.

CHAPTER IX

PLANS INTERRUPTED

Upon reaching Ashwood we ran into Yndra's dark spire and up the stairs with our weapons drawn. A magical barrier kept us from entering the room where the identical women held Takarha captive. I swung my sword against the shimmering, transparent wall to no avail.

"No. No," one of the devilish women said, waving a finger. Placing her hands against the barrier, she licked it with her black, forked tongue, taunting us.

"Ambros and the lovely Eleanor," the other Yndra greeted us with a smile. "You made it just in time." She took hold of two wooden handles that had been attached to the top of the obsidian egg and removed the heavy lid as if it weighed nothing.

"I don't believe I like you anymore," Lorena told them. Looking at Takarha, who was lying bound and gagged on the floor, she asked, "Are you all right, sweetie?"

She shook her head that she wasn't.

"Vampires are physically unaffected by time," Yndra began. She pulled a rope down from a system of pulleys and hooked it to the shackles around Takarha's ankles. She hoisted the squirming girl over the open egg. "There are few things that can truly destroy them, save dragon breath or decapitation." She picked up a sword from the table and rubbed her thumb over its edge to feel the sharpness.

"You don't mean to kill this little girl?" I questioned.

Answering with a devilish smile, "I am curing her."

"You're stealing her immortality to give to your baby," I argued. "You told me that you meant to eradicate your kind."

"And how do you suppose I survive against them? This little girl holds the key to tipping the balance of power."

"Only in your favor," I interjected.

"Your father foresaw this shift in power."

I hit the mystical barrier with my fist. "Do not use my pop to justify your actions!"

"Oh, I struck a nerve," she ridiculed. "I may take this petite form to walk amongst your people, but I am much too large to gain immortality from this girl. My duplicate, however, is still small enough to benefit from her blood."

"But won't she be unable to age?" Lorena asked. "She will remain a child just as Takarha has."

"My studies have shown that it will take much

longer for her blood to alter the body completely, plenty of time for her to reach adulthood. I will then wage war against the World Council, exterminate the dragon races, and rule over the humans unmatched forever," she boasted.

Pointing to the infant dragon suspended within the egg, I explained to her, "That dragon may attain immortality, but you and your guardian here will die. You will never see if your progeny completes your quest."

With a grin spreading across her face, she explained, "Ah, but my guardian isn't just a copy of me; she is me. Like this child dragon, our minds are the same. We share the same thoughts. Another body is merely an extension of my reach, not a separate entity. You can thank your pop for that."

"You're taking Pop's work and twisting it to suit your own devious plans."

"I am merely—"

Screams from outside brought an abrupt end to our conversation. Yndra ran to the window and grunted her disapproval. "Why does this have to happen, now?" She walked over to us and removed the magical barrier between us. She held her hands up as if surrendering. "We don't have time for all this squabbling; we need to work together if we're to save Ashwood."

"What's going on?"

"We're being attacked. Come on."

We followed her downstairs and outside to see an army of undead attacking the city!

"Are these the vampires that you melted?" Lorena asked Yndra.

"No, these are different," the one standing behind us answered. "These have been summoned."

"Then we must find the summoner," I announced, charging into the thick of battle.

Zombies and skeletons poured into the city like a mass of hungry cannibals. The elves tried holding them back from completely overrunning the city, but it was clear there were too many to hold back for long.

The two sultry dragon women didn't take their large serpentine forms but had black wings extend from their backs. They flew close to their targets so not to spit their deadly toxin on the elves they were protecting.

The elves shot enchanted arrows that produced a variety of effects. Some froze their target completely in ice before shattering them into many pieces. Others caused the target to catch fire that was so hot they burned to ash in mere moments. There were arrows that pierced several targets, creating a magical tether that drew them together. Some arrows were powerful enough to break the hold the summoner had over his minions, causing them to turn against the others or even collapse where they stood.

The zombies were best dispatched by severing the brain from the body, but the skeleton warriors were resurrected using a different spell. Although it wasn't seen, I knew dark magic held their bones together. Detaching them wasn't enough since they could reattach them. Their bones had to be made unusable or their magic dispelled.

The enchantments my swords possessed were of no use against these monsters since they had no circulating blood for the curses to take effect. I attempted to turn three sword wielding skeletons that surrounded me with a thought, but the magic binding them was too powerful.

"Looks like I'll have to do this one at a time," I said while defending myself from attacks.

I plunged my swords into the ground to free up my hands. I grabbed the arm of one of the skeletons and forced him against the side of a house where I sent a powerful thought into his bones. I saw the necromancer who resurrected it, and he saw me! He was a Dark Elf! "It cannot be!" I gasped and fell away from the skeleton. It was Pop! I saw Ambrosius! Or more precisely, I saw Byron, the man from the journal I read at the World Council Palace.

I retrieved my swords and severed limbs only for the skeletons to reattach them. I then decapitated them one by one. I sheathed my swords and snatched up their skulls, juggling them while staying just out of their reach.

"I have your heads. I have your heads," I teased. "Want them back, do you?" I asked while laughing at the sight of three headless skeletons clumsily grasping for their skulls.

I let a skull slip past my hand, and I kicked it off into the distance. "There it goes!" I announced, and one of the skeletons scurried off to retrieve it.

I jammed the other two skulls under the ribs of the skeletons, cracking some of them in the process. They attacked each other to retrieve their head.

I ran to Lorena, who was holding her ground against approaching zombies not far from me, showing great skill with the blade. The enchantment on her sword didn't affect them either, but she didn't let that slow her down.

I pulled her away from the fighting. "While

Yndra is distracted, we should go back to free Takarha."

She nodded her approval of the plan, so, with no opposition between us and the black tower, we hurried back.

I opened the tower doors to find the obsidian egg broken from the bottom, the unborn dragon dead on the floor in a puddle of the milky white, magical elixir. We could hear someone upstairs.

I motioned for Lorena to stay there for a moment, and I quietly made my way upstairs. Takarha was lying on the floor, still bound and gagged. There was a pale, dark-haired man filling a satchel with things from Yndra's long table. The necromancer who commanded the army of undead was also there. He was leaning over the opened obsidian egg, examining its construction.

"It's you," I blurted out, startling the two intruders.

The man at the table turned quickly, throwing a telekinetic force at me, but I shielded myself from the energy. Getting a better look at him, I recognized the human from my childhood.

"Dirk, why have you brought war upon us?" I asked, shocked that he had returned to Ashwood with an army.

"No offense, but I'm here to rid the world of your race," he spat bitterly.

"But Dirk, don't you remember me? I'm Ambros, Eve's friend."

"Then you should not have come back."

He leaped at me, conjuring a glaive from the ethereal plane to strike me down. My swords blocked the fearsome weapon, but he took me off balance and kicked me down the stairs.

"Ambros!" I heard Lorena yell while I tumbled down the stairs.

Dirk leaped from the top step to attack me before I could get up, but Lorena was there to protect me. The strength behind Dirk's swing pushed the tip of her blade to floor next to me. Their weapons were so close to me, I was afraid to breathe.

"This doesn't concern you, woman," Dirk announced, holding his glaive against her sword.

"You hurt my friend, and I'll—" KA-POW! Lorena punched Dirk right in the mouth. "—kick your white ass," she finished the warning, her eyes burning with anger.

Blood oozed from the edge of a smile cracking across Dirk's face. "I believe you're a keeper," he commented, licking the blood from his mouth. "But I'll have to get back to you about courtship." He then extended an open hand and magically threw her against the wall!

During that brief moment Dirk was distracted, I grabbed my swords and rolled out of reach of his ethereal glaive. Back on my feet, I made a quick glance at Lorena to see that she was only stunned by the push before having to defend myself from Dirk's relentless attacks.

Lorena soon returned to the fight, but Dirk held us both off with his bladed staff. After blocking both of my swords, he spun around and knocked Lorena's sword from her hand. Before he could bring his staff around to defend himself, I sliced up, splitting his chin and lips with Scourge, the green sword of insanity. He instantly lost concentration on his weapon, causing it to leave this world, and he voiced a terrible scream. He grabbed Lorena with an unseen hand while she was retrieving her sword and hurled her and it into me. The red obsidian sword pierced my right shoulder. Its powerful enchantment caused the blood surrounding the blade to have a violent reaction, and my shoulder exploded, dislodging the sword!

I howled in agony and fell to the floor, my cries quickly turning to grueling laughter. I saw Byron rush down the stairs carrying a thick book and a glass orb. Holding the orb out to us, a magical barrier formed around me and Lorena, blocking Dirk's attacks against us.

"I want to take them back with us," I heard Byron say to Dirk, but he continued to punch the force field that imprisoned us. Ripples spread across the surface from the points of impact. Byron slid his book into a satchel and placed his hand on Dirk's shoulder. "Calm yourself." And he immediately began to relax. "I cannot use this dragon to break the spell holding Magnus. We must get out of the city; our army won't distract them for much longer."

Within the magical sphere, Lorena held me while she cried. "Don't you die on me, now."

"What a delightful phrase," I said to her as my vision began to blur. "You know, I can't think of a better place to die than on you."

She laughed through her tears. "I think I've become a bad influence on you."

I reached up to feel the damage done to my shoulder and found that my right arm was completely gone. The damage was so extensive, I could feel a lung beyond broken ribs!

"Oh, don't touch it," I heard her say, pulling my hand away.

Her face drew close, and I felt her lips touch mine. And then, I lost consciousness.

CHAPTER X

A SADISTIC JOKE

"Will he become one of us?" I heard a cold voice ask.

"I hope so," another voice spoke out from the darkness.

"He looks absolutely delectable."

"QUIET! HE'S WAKING UP," many voices said in unison.

My eyes opened to find myself in a chamber illuminated by small magical orbs that gave off wonderful green light. The orbs were held by skeletal hands that extended from the walls. My wrists were shackled and chains held my arms out. I hung naked, chest-deep in a large cauldron of blood set into the floor. The walls, floor, and ceiling were completely covered in a mass of corpses that whispered to one another.

"This place is wonderful!" I said aloud, wide-eyed and excited. I then remembered that I had lost my right arm, but it was back as if nothing had happened to it. "This must be the afterlife. I must have died."

"YOU DID DIE, AND YOU CAME TO US," the undead that surrounded me answered.

"When I came here, was a woman with me?"

"SHE WAS SACRIFICED TO HELA."

"What? I need to see her! Release me!" I ordered them, pulling at my chains. "Please, let me see her."

"WE MUSTN'T. THE KING COMMANDED US TO WATCH OVER YOU WHILE HE'S GONE."

"And who, may I ask, is your king?"

"WHY KING BYRON, OF COURSE," they answered.

"Ah, I've met him. Is he a Dark Elf from the city of Ashwood?" I asked, curious why he looked exactly like my pop but goes by the name Byron.

"That body was gifted to him by Magnus the Red," one of the skeletons answered.

"Does Magnus still live, or is he somewhere in this wonderful afterlife, too?" I asked, already knowing he was cast into the Abyss of the Dead, but I wanted them to tell me what they knew.

"HE LIVES. A POWERFUL SPELL HAS INPRISONED HIM DEEP WITHIN THE EARTH. ONLY A WORTHY SACRIFICE WILL FREE HIM."

"And what would make a worthy sacrifice?"

"A DRAGON, BUT NOT A BLACK ONE, NO. A BLACK DRAGON WILL NOT DO."

"Where is the King, now? Is he out looking for a different kind of dragon?"

One spoke out, "No, he left to speak with Magnus who dwells within the dwarven..."

"SHH, HERE SHE COMES!" the others interrupted.

"Who? Who's coming?"

The undead wall divided, allowing a woman to enter. It was Lorena! She calmly strolled into the room, her beauty all the more potent against a backdrop of corpses.

"Lorena, you're alive! I was afraid you had been killed. They said you had been sacrificed. Or are we both dead, spending eternity together in this paradise?"

"What else did those useless imbeciles say to you?" she questioned, her tone ringing stern, cold, ghostly.

Something terrible had been done to her. Had she been poisoned? Is she under a spell? I finally asked her what was wrong.

By raising her hand, my chains lifted me out of the pool and eye level with her. Blood from the pool dripped from my naked body. She stepped closer, and I could see her head was crowned with stitches. "I am not your beloved Lorena. I am Queen Hela, and you will address me as such."

Knowing something had been done to her felt like a punch in the stomach. "No," I coughed. I raised my head and gasped for breath.

She floated over the small pool of blood and felt of my shoulder. "It appears you have mended well. My husband will be pleased." Her hand slid down my stomach, and she whispered seductively, "But I believe I will enjoy your body more than he."

She turned quickly to leave the room. "Say nothing to him," she ordered the dead. "And change these lights!"

The green-lit orbs immediately turned to white, and the bones shifted to close off the doorway. "WE DON'T LIKE HER," the dead announced. "SHE'S A TWISTED, EVIL QUEEN."

Hanging from my chains, I took a deep breath of the cold, stale air. "Well, since I'm here, I suppose I should introduce myself. My name is Ambros."

The bones that covered the walls moved to allow more and more skulls to reach the surface. "WE'RE NOT SUPPOSED TO TALK TO YOU."

Ignoring the command they were given, I told them with a nod, "I'm pleased to meet you all."

"HE'S PLEASED TO MEET US!" the skulls said happily to one another.

"May I have your names?" I asked of the countless undead that surrounded me.

The skulls turned to look at those around them. "NAMES? NAMES. DO WE HAVE NAMES?"

"I believe I can help you remember who you are," I told them. "Can one of you step forward?"

The walls began rolling like the sea, and the magical orbs that lit the room bobbled along the surface causing the room to dim and brighten. A single skeleton finally pulled free of the mass. Rising from the floor to stand tall, its bones were thick. The magic that held it together created a green aura that emanated from its joints. It wore bits of ancient armor, tarnished and dented. It wielded a large, rusty battle axe with a bone handle and kneeled before me. I suddenly saw, not a skeleton, but a man kneeling before me. The room was quiet, and I looked into his old bones.

"You were a great warrior in life, a general in Byron's army. You had a wife and three sons. You died in service defending Byron's keep against the dragon army. Your name was and always will be Galenos."

He stood and looked at me with his cold, empty eye sockets. For a brief moment, I caught a glimpse of him as a living man again, and he was shedding tears. With a nod of his head, he stepped back into the wall.

Another skeleton gathered its parts to step forward. It stood naked with its hands clasped together, quietly waiting for me to speak. This one was much smaller than Galenos, and I saw her, too, as a healthy, living person. She was a pretty, young girl.

"Odilia," I saw her name immediately. I suddenly felt fear and took a deep breath to remind myself that it was an old memory hardened within this creature's bones. "I see you being led against your will to a courtyard filled with broken stones. You were sacrificed by your people to winged creatures known as Strigoi, an ancient race of vampires that guarded this castle."

Odilia covered her expressionless face and returned to the wall.

For hours, I spoke to each and every skeleton that stepped forward from the wall of corpses. Most of the armor-clad skeletons died while fighting dragons alongside Galenos. Some were the King's servants. Others were taken from their homes in nearby villages.

I felt overwhelmed by the lives they lived, bringing tears to my eyes. Recognizing the scent, I tasted the tears that streamed down my face to find they were blood. "What's happened to me?"

"You've been healed," a skull with a twisted jaw announced.

"HELA RETURNS," they warned.

"Open this room!" I heard her command.

The bones shifted to create a hall leading into the room. The woman in possession of Lorena's body floated into the room, not wearing Lorena's clothes, but an extravagant, green dress.

"So what do you think?" she asked, turning around to show me the back.

Thinking it would be best to play along, I answered, "You look gorgeous, but I feel a bit overdressed." I glanced down at my naked, bloodstained body.

She floated over and rubbed her hands over my stomach and up my chest. "You're perfect just the way you are."

She then kissed me harder than Lorena ever did, leaving my lip bleeding from a bite. Her nails tore at my back. "I can't wait until Byron returns and possesses your body. I want you, now." She kissed me again, tasting the blood she had drawn.

"Mmm. How 'bout you take these chains off," I suggested, trying to sweet talk her into freeing me.

"Why?" she grinned. "Do you prefer working with your hands?"

She reached around and smacked my ass, leaving it with a good sting.

"Oh yeah. Here we go. Punish me, hotness. I've been a bad elf. Release these chains and have your way with me."

"I most certainly will," she warned seductively. "But the chains stay on."

"Well, it was worth a try."

She slid the straps of her dress off her shoulders to let it fall away from her curvaceous, tan body. "I'm going to put a hurting on you, you won't soon forget."

She wrapped her arms around me and began kissing and biting my neck. Extending a hand, she telekinetically pulled a rusty dagger from the wall of undead. "I love the smell of fresh blood," she confessed, plunging the knife in my back, between my ribs, and pulling it around my chest.

Puncturing a lung, I gasped for breath.

"Do I take your breath away?" she whispered. "Don't worry; you'll heal," she told me, kissing down my chest to the blood oozing from the wound. "And I will remain young and beautiful forever."

"NO!" a rumbling voice swelled from all around. "WE HATE YOU, WITCH!" the dead walls yelled. "YOU MADE US FORGET WHO WE WERE! YOU CHAINED US TO THIS WORLD, IMPRISONED US WITHIN THIS MOUNTAIN, BOUND US TO THESE BONES AGAINST OUR WILL! YOU AND YOUR KING WILL NOT RULE OVER US ANY LONGER!"

The white light emitting from the magical orbs turned red, and the bones that covered the walls boiled with hatred. Swords and spears extended all around us, and the room began closing in.

Looking around at the enclosing blades, I began to laugh.

Hela yelled back at them. "I am your queen, and you will serve me! You will do my bidding! You will…"

"DIE!" the walls roared.

The shackles that held me unlatched, and I dropped into the pool of blood. I was unable to see within the dark liquid, but I could hear chaos above me and feel the turmoil through my body. I reached out for something to grab hold but felt nothing. I could not breathe but felt no need for air.

The roar swelled like an approaching tornado and then suddenly went silent. A boney hand found mine and pulled me from the pool. I found the room was back to the way it was. The skeleton that helped me withdrew into the ceiling.

"Where's Lorena?" I questioned.

"THAT WAS NOT HER," they reminded me.

"Then where's Hela?"

"WE TOOK HER," the room answered. "SHE IS PART OF US, NOW."

"Not one of us," a single voice spoke.

"But used for parts," another clarified.

I was naked and dripping with blood. I magically created a towel to dry myself off, but it only smeared the blood that covered me. "Ugh, this won't do," I uttered.

Many arms reached out to me. "YOU HELPED US REMEMBER WHO WE ARE. LET US HELP YOU."

I held my arm out to them, and I was pulled down into the floor! My body was pushed, twisted, and pulled in the cold darkness among the dead. I was then slowly dropped from the ceiling, so I could land on my feet. The blood that covered me was cleared away, and, although they were rough with me, I saw no cuts or bruises. I then concentrated to create a new set of clothing for myself.

The stone floor was cold beneath my bare feet, so I began by magically forming a thick pair of boots. I designed them to look and feel like the fur boots the Dark Elves wore. I then created a pair of black pants and a thick, sleeveless shirt. I felt much better, except for an aching hunger. I sat on the edge of the pool for a moment, suddenly lightheaded.

Holding my stomach, I asked the dead surrounding me, "Do you happen to have a sniff of cheese or a crust of bread?"

"Sniff? Crust? Whatever do you mean?" a skull with a nasally voice asked. "We have neither of those things down here in the dark."

Catching the scent of the blood that filled the pool behind me, I examined my hands and suddenly realized what had been done to me. "It cannot be! What is this, some sort of sadistic joke? I've been changed."

"WE TOLD YOU. WE TOLD YOU THAT YOU'VE BEEN HEALED."

I scooped up a palmful of blood from the pool and smelled of it. The blood didn't smell the way it used to; it smelled sweet. I sipped it, and my body craved more. I had tasted blood before, during my necromantic studies, but I remembered it having a distinct metallic taste. Now, it had a taste similar to warm honey. I drank until I no longer felt the hunger pangs.

"ARE YOU FEELING BETTER, SIR?"

"Yes, thank you. Do you think maybe I can leave, now?"

"OH! OH! YES!"

The walls shifted to reveal a corridor leading to another room. I ran into a larger chamber to find bloody instruments and a clay jar on a table. I could sense dead matter within the jar, so I opened it, finding a brain. I pulled the brain out and held it, feeling its memories through my fingertips. Tears of blood began streaming down my face again.

"It's her," I murmured. "Oh, I'm so sorry, Lorena."

I saw a memory of myself through Lorena's eyes when I was unconscious in Ashwood. She would never admit it, but she did love me. She held me in our magical prison as it shrunk us down to fit within the orb that Byron carried. Takarha was also held prisoner within the orb. Byron and Dirk blended in as defenders of Ashwood by attacking their own army while making their way to the tunnel leading out of the city. Summoning spectral steeds, they rode to this place where Byron used us in his dark experiments. He used the knowledge he learned from my father's notes and every drop of Takarha's blood to create the rejuvenating pool. I was his test subject to find out whether or not the magical elixir mixed with the blood of a vampire would turn me into one. Lorena was chained to this table where Byron removed her brain and replaced it with his queen's to give her a new, beautiful body.

I carefully placed Lorena's brain back into the clay jar and sat on the edge of the table to think.

"We're sorry about your friends," I heard the skeleton Odilia say. Her voice was a chilling whisper in the cold room.

I looked around at the many skeletons. They had divided and taken shape while I was lost in Lorena's memories.

"Friends," I repeated. Sensing she was still here, I called, "Takarha!"

The elfling stepped out from the undead wall. Her flesh was dry and sunken much like Kronyx when Jinxie stabbed him with Devour. I got down on my knees and hugged her.

"Look what he did to me, Ambros," she said sadly, pulling her head free from her body. "He only wanted my blood, the blood Eve gave me," her now disembodied head explained.

"I'm sorry, Takarha."

"It's okay. I have a new family, now," she said, lifting her head up to smile at the undead surrounding us.

"Is there anything I can do for you?" I offered.

Placing her head back in its proper place, she answered, "Eve's gift of eternal life now flows through your veins. Don't waste it. Don't waste it," she repeated.

I cried and held her again before she rejoined the others.

"Goodbye, my dear Takarha."

Now that I was a vampire, I felt my powers were enhanced, for I could sense the remains of horses and even more dead soldiers far above us near the surface of the underground temple.

"Odilia, where is your king?" I asked again. "Where is Byron?"

"He and Master Dirk have gone to the dwarven kingdom."

"Can you lead me to this kingdom?"

"We can," Galenos answered. His voice was shrill and frightening. "Byron commanded us to watch over you, so that's exactly what we're going to do. We may be twisting his orders, but he can still press his will against us. If we turn on you, it is not our doing."

"I understand."

"Centurions! Prepare to depart!" the ancient, undead general commanded.

A hunched back skeleton wearing only a helmet

asked, "Do we have to do it outside?"

"We cannot travel that distance in one night. The sun will destroy us!" another spoke out, bringing others to voice their disapproval of leaving the safety of their dark sanctuary.

I waved my hand to silence them. "You've grown too comfortable down here in the mountain. The sun will not destroy you, but it may destroy me," I added, remembering Eve telling me years ago that the sun burned her skin. "How far is the entrance to the dwarven kingdom?"

"It is a three day's ride. We can leave at dusk and cover a lot of ground before dawn," Galenos answered.

"Good. Does the sun shine, now?" I asked since I had lost track of time.

"It's not yet mid-day, Lord Ambros."

"Thank you. In the meantime, why don't you all head to the surface, so you can feel the sun on your old bones while you call your horses from their slumber?"

"We have horses?" I heard someone ask excitedly.

The undead soldiers marched out of the room toward the entrance while I looked around their king's sanctuary. With the walls now bare of bones, the place seemed much larger. I walked into a room where its walls and ceiling were layered in bits of parchment and dried skins with writings on them. In the center of the room was a stone pedestal holding the glass orb that I was captured in. It illuminated the room in a soft light.

Stone steps led up to a sarcophagus large enough for two. A scene of people worshipping a great dragon was carved into it.

Against the left wall, there was a writing desk with a large book under another glowing orb. I sat down at the desk and saw that the book was Byron's journal. I flipped to the beginning to find out who he was before taking my father's body. I was amazed how the dark blood that now coursed through my veins allowed me to read much quicker than I ever had before.

What I learned was that near the end of the Draconian Wars, the days of peace began to return under Shadowrath's solitary rule. Giants, trolls, goblins, even dragons, what few remained, pledged their allegiance, but their lives meant nothing to him, for he preferred the dead over the living. All creatures that once lived were summoned to carry out his commands. But there remained one he feared could overthrow his reign—Arethil, the last phoenix of this world. Before marching his army against her, he devised a plan in case he was to perish. He molded dead flesh over the bones of a fallen elf and breathed undead life into his creation. He named him Byron and bestowed upon him a portion of his terrible power for the sole purpose of reviving him.

As Shadowrath's immense army marched on the Evergreen Plains, home of the elves, Byron awaited his master's call in the Citadel of Shadow. Once news reached his ear that Arethil sacrificed herself to defeat Shadowrath, Byron commanded a second army of undead to reclaim the great dragon's remains. But it was Shadowrath's living followers that destroyed his army before his ultimate demise. All those who valued their life and the life of their kin turned against Shadowrath and stood alongside the elves to defeat Byron's undead army.

The weight of the Draconian Wars was lifted, but all races felt defeated. With the light of Arethil extinguished, the Great Winter spread from the north to blanket the world in ice. Many dragons struggled for supremacy once again, while others decided it was best to allow their race time to recover from the brink of extinction. These dragons formed an alliance and vowed to rebuild a peaceful world and live closely with the elves during this new age when the earth itself seemed bent on purging itself of life.

The elves wished for Arethil's return, but the risk of Shadowrath's resurrection was much too great. The Dragons, on the other hand, did not want either to exist in their world because both entities posed a threat. After much debate, an obsidian chest was forged and powerful magic was used to hold both Arethil and Shadowrath within a dimensional prison. The chest was then cast into the Abyss of the Dead, along with many of the fallen, never to be brought back to the surface.

No longer with purpose, Byron disappeared into the wilderness. For centuries, he studied himself and what creatures crossed his path until one day, he came upon a small village of people similar to the elves. His dead skin made it impossible to pass as one of them, so he remained in shadow and studied them from a distance. Once he realized they were unskilled with magic and barely capable of surviving the harsh climate, he stepped out of the darkness. The men of the tribe moved to attack him, but Byron called upon the remains of animals that the people had killed for food. Hundreds of skeletons arose from the snow and joined together to form a bone golem. The frightened warriors lowered their spears and bowed down to Byron, along with the rest of the villagers.

To better withstand the cold, Byron led his people into the mountains and into a system of caves that he had discovered in his travels. He then asked the mightiest among them to offer himself as a sacrifice. The man gave himself willingly, and Byron breathed his life into the man. He transferred his consciousness into the man's body to appear as one of them, to feel alive for the first time in his long life.

From among the flourishing city within the mountain, Byron took a woman as his queen. Her name was Hela, and she was both strong and beautiful. She worked closely with her people while Byron experimented and delved deeper into the arcane.

Through Byron's magic, his people grew to be very old. After their passing, he brought them back to continue serving him and the living. But the real honor was being chosen as the king and queen's new vessel. With every century that passed, Byron and Hela chose a new body from among their citizens.

The Great Winter finally came to an end, and the ice receded north, allowing for Byron's people to live above ground once again. A castle was built on the mountain where they had lived for millennia. The living began building homes for their growing families farther and farther away, while the dead were called to the castle to spend their afterlife in service to their king, defending his kingdom from the multitude of beasts that roamed the lands.

Byron ruled over a prosperous kingdom. That was until a new threat came upon the wind. Though, it wasn't another ice age to envelop the world. It was a dragon! A Red Dragon from the east, with a taste for human flesh, burned homes and devoured people.

Byron and his army of both living and dead soldiers attacked the great serpent with arrows and spears. They lured the dragon away from the homes to the castle. It broke down the doors, and while taking the form of an elf, it stormed in to see what king would cower behind the throne while his cities burned. But Byron did not cower. He called forth a flood of undead from the depths of the castle to force the beast back outside where they merged to form a massive golem. The dragon returned to its true form and fought the golem before taking to the air to flee.

Homes were rebuilt, and the living felt safe again while their deceased ancestors kept unblinking eyes on the kingdom's ever-expanding borders. Peace had returned, but it was not to last.

From the east, a storm blew that shook the very walls of Byron's keep. The dragon had returned but, this time, with others carrying giants on their backs! Byron's great kingdom was reduced to ash, and his army of undead was destroyed by fire and lightning. Byron and his queen, along with what few families escaped, retreated back into the ancient tunnels of the mountain.

Leaving Hela to watch over their people, Byron journeyed east to learn that the race of dragons had grown strong. They claimed to serve the elves, but, in secret, they drew plans against them and used the lesser creatures to set their scheme into motion. The elves were kept divided, weak, while the dragons' numbers grew. The dragons of the council believed it was nearing time to strike.

Upon meeting him, Byron knew Magnus was undead. He knew he was a type of vampire, but an opportunity to study him didn't arise until now. It seemed Magnus survived his decent into the abyss, and he sent word to Dirk that he was imprisoned and residing in the dwarven kingdom until the spell could be broken. He also sent word that he had recovered the chest containing Arethil's remains. A band of dwarves attempted to bring it to Dirk and Byron, but they were killed by goblins before reaching the surface.

Magnus instructed Dirk to locate the lost chest and carry it to the surface where direct sunlight will revive Arethil, and the race of dragons can be vanquished forever. While Arethil is capable of creating herself a new body, Byron fears he will be called by Shadowrath to give up his to hold the immense power of his master within this world. Byron has lived many ages, now, and doesn't wish to give up his existence.

Byron believes he can break the spell on Magnus, but he needs the mystical properties found only in the blood of a dragon. From what race of dragon, he doesn't yet know. The sample taken from the infant Black Dragon in Ashwood ruled out their blood. While he continues to search for a dragon that he can capture easily, he plans to release Magnus only after he has taken the chest for himself. He wants to study its contents without releasing its prisoners in hopes of siphoning the power from within.

Scattered throughout his journal, Byron drew strange symbols that glowed various colors to the trained eye. Rubbing a finger over the symbols, I could feel a pulsing energy that sent visions into my mind. It was a list of spells he had learned and created over the centuries! There were spells on raising and controlling the dead. There were many spells learned from an enchanted staff called the Staff of Storms. A spell to summon weapons made of ethereal energy was learned from Dirk. There were also many pages with detailed drawings of creatures that he had seen in his travels and experimented on.

His experiment on me was a success. He intended to use the blood of a vampire to heal his own body so that he wouldn't have to continue transferring his consciousness into another. He had learned from my father's notes in Ashwood that he could replicate a small sample of blood to the amount he needed.

I read all that he had written, learning everything before I felt it was time to leave.

CHAPTER XI

WAR IN THE EARTH

My swords, Scourge and Devour, were on another table. I strapped them to my back and carried the clay jar containing Lorena's brain up a long tunnel that led into a ruined castle. The roof had long since collapsed, but the rubble had been pushed aside to create a path outside. The skeletons were standing shoulder to shoulder, filling the courtyard, staring up at the darkening sky. The sun had fallen below the tree line, making the green glow of their joints look as though a strange mist had descended on the hillside.

I saw no horses. I could feel they were still buried in the earth. I took a seat on a block of stone in the courtyard of the castle and waited until the undead army watched the last rays of sunlight fade into the shadow of night.

When the dead turned to face me, I ordered

them, pointing at the dirt beneath my feet, "I want all of Lorena's remains right here."

One by one, they stepped forward, and, without argument, they removed bones from their bodies that once belonged to the charismatic captain and placed them at my feet. The last skeleton to approach took hold of its skull and popped it free from its spine before gently placing it on the pile of freshly stripped bones.

I knelt next to the remains to examine the skull. The stitching used to hold the top in place was broken, and Hela's brain had been removed. I took Lorena's brain from the jar and placed it within the skull. For a moment, I thought of resurrecting her, but I knew she would be disgusted without flesh. While standing among the quietly waiting dead, I finally decided it was best to let her go. With a snap of my fingers, Lorena's remains burst into flames.

The skeletons made a strange hissing noise that caused the ground to shake. The decomposed bodies of hundreds of horses stood up beneath their rider. They were held together by the same green aura. As quickly as they were summoned, they began riding out of the courtyard. I called for a horse of my own and followed the army east.

Skeletal horses can travel much faster than live ones, so we swept across the land quickly. During the day, I found that the sun did in fact burn my skin, so I wore enough clothing to protect myself from the light.

After three days, we reached a castle built on the side of a volcano.

"Nice place," I commented.

We dismounted our horses, and I broke open the large castle doors with a magical force. Inside, twelve human guards brandishing spears rushed to stop us. "HALT!" they ordered.

The army of undead charged past me to quickly dismember them, and I strolled inside to meet a regal gentleman standing at the throne. "What is this madness you've brought here?" he yelled at me. "I am Artimes, chief architect of this castle, and I demand to know why you've come with these, these corpses."

Without a word, I continued walking toward him. He drew his sword, but I telekinetically tossed it from his hand. I grabbed hold of him, and with the thirst burning inside me once again, I bit into the man's neck. From his mind, I saw that Byron hired him to build a castle over a tunnel that goblins used to gain entry into the dwarven kingdom. Artimes was to hold the throne until Magnus could be released.

I withdrew my teeth from Artimes' neck, and he fell back against the steps of the throne. It was strange drinking blood from the living, but I needed it after three days without any.

More soldiers charged in from hallways leading into the throne room, but their weapons were useless at killing those that were already dead. My army made short work of them, and I brought them all back to serve me. I led them down long corridors and stairs into the depths of the castle where more guards were stationed at a barred door leading into the caverns.

"Stand aside, soldiers," I ordered. "Or become one of these guys." I pointed a thumb over my shoulder to my followers.

The guards stepped aside and stood quietly, shaking in their boots while I unbarred the door and hundreds of skeletons marched past them into the dark tunnels.

The dead laughed at the men. "You will be joining our ranks soon enough," some said, patting the men on the shoulder as they passed.

"Once you're dead, you'll no longer fear us," others said.

While I stood with the guards, waiting for the last of my army to enter the caverns, I heard strange squawks coming from within. The guards whispered, "Goblins!"

I commanded them to bar the door once we get inside. They nodded that they understood, so I followed my army into the cavern. The large, thick doors were shut and barred behind me. Many of the soldiers raised torches that burst into green flame as they marched down the large tunnel that led deeper and deeper into the earth.

There were many tunnels leading off from the main one, but far ahead, I could hear the clash of swords. "Let me get to the front," I told them, and they separated for me to pass through. I ran through the tunnel, finding a group of dead goblins along the way. They were about three feet tall with long, pointy noses and ears. They wore leather and animal furs. Some had mossy-green skin while others had dull brown skin.

I took a moment to call them up to join me on my quest. I saw nothing in their minds of the obsidian chest that was supposedly lost within these caves, but I did find that some were dead before we got here. I saw Byron and Dirk within their minds. I should kill them both, but if Pop knew his body would be reused after his death, perhaps Byron has it for a reason.

With six undead goblins standing before me in the tunnel as my soldiers marched by us, I assigned them with a special mission. "Goblins, I have reason to believe a black chest is somewhere in these tunnels. I need you to recover it for me. Do you understand?"

The goblins raised their tiny spears and squawked that they understood their orders. They climbed on top of my soldiers to hop quickly over them through the tunnels in search of the chest.

Many other dead goblins littered the dark tunnel, killed by Byron and Dirk as they passed through. Now in death, they joined my army.

I raced on to the frontlines where my army was battling another small group of goblins. The diminutive creatures stood no chance against us, but they fought fiercely nonetheless until the tunnels became quiet. Either the remaining goblins retreated into the side tunnels, or they have all been killed.

The deeper we marched, the hotter it became. I began to feel a constant vibration beneath my feet. I held up my hand to stop the army that I led. I placed a hand against the floor and then to the wall of the tunnel to feel the very life force of the earth flowing just beyond the rock. It was a wonderful feeling, yet unnerving at the same time. Only a few feet of rock separated us from incinerating lava!

Not far ahead, I felt that I passed through a magical barrier of some sort, but it had no effect on me.

"We're getting close," I informed those behind me before continuing deeper into the earth.

A fragrance reached my nostrils that reminded me of evening meals with Pop. "Mmm, I smell ham," I said aloud before coming upon a pile of scorched goblin corpses, and it was clear that the smell of ham came from their burnt flesh. "Goblins! BLUGH!"

We finally reached a heavy door that was barred from the other side. I used my telekinetic power to unbar it. Beyond the door was an immense chamber where we were met by Dirk and an army of zombie dwarves!

Throughout the chamber were many large, widely spaced columns that appeared to be made of obsidian. Volcanic magma flowed through them to both illuminate and heat the room.

Dirk stood at the forefront of the army wielding an ethereal glaive like the one he used in Ashwood. He wore leather armor with a bronze chest plate.

"It pleases me to announce that your journey has reached its end."

"You know, Dick, I think I'd like you better dead," I laughed, unsheathing my swords.

"Smash them into dust!" Dirk ordered his heavily armored troops.

Dirk leaped at me to attack, and the two zombie armies crashed together like waves in a raging sea around us. I was a vampire, now, so my reaction speed was much quicker than when we last fought.

An undead dwarf stepped in to attack me with his war hammer. Swinging my swords, I severed both his and the hammer's head. "Those looked important."

Dirk began laughing. "I drank from you before Byron began his experiment. Ambrosius, your naïve father, died for nothing; you will never bring back your dead girlfriend, Jinxie; Magnus will soon be released from the earth; and the rest of your wretched race will burn!"

I have never been one to anger easily, but his

words struck a nerve deep within my soul, and rage took me. I fought harder, carelessly. My attacks were easily deflected as he toyed with me.

"Oh! I nearly forgot about the whore. I drank from her, too, before Byron sawed off her head. Her blood was the sweetest I've ever tasted," Dirk taunted, licking his lips.

"I WANT YOU DEAD!" I screamed, attacking wildly.

He blocked my attacks and knocked both Scourge and Devour from my hands. They struck one of the large columns and fell to floor. He kicked me in the face, and I fell. He attempted to impale me, but I summoned a shield in time to block the attack and a spear to counter attack.

Stepping out of reach, he nodded his head, saying, "I'm impressed."

I quickly got back on my feet, but a bony hand took hold of my shoulder and pulled me into the crowd. It was Odilia.

"You're going to retreat?" I heard Dirk yell. "Come back here and die like you're supposed to!"

Patiently, I asked, "What's wrong, Odilia?"

"We're not doing well," she informed me.

It was then that I noticed one of her arms had been smashed, and the war raging around us wasn't tipping in my favor. The dwarves were better equipped, and my soldiers were losing limbs faster than they could reattach them.

A dwarf swung his axe at me only to bang against my ethereal shield. I pushed him away and summoned my army to create a circle around me.

"We cannot win this war," Odilia told me.

Once a perimeter was formed, I placed my spear and shield on the stone floor long enough to cut my hand on one of the many broken swords. While I could still hear Dirk yelling over the clashing battle, I marked the floor with my blood but nothing happened.

"DAMN!" I cursed, striking the floor with my bloody fist. "Byron's resurrection spell is too powerful for me to take control of them."

Looking up to Odilia, I thought of an even better spell to cast. While my hand still bled, I drew a second character on the floor that brought the dead to silence throughout the entire chamber, and my army began merging like the walls they formed beneath Byron's castle. Only this time, they formed one massive creature—a bone golem! Odilia was soon pulled into the growing hulk to add to its frightening mass.

"Bones, exterminate them!" I commanded.

The dwarves stood motionless as they looked up to their, now enormous, adversary. The golem lifted its heavy foot and stomped three dwarves at once, absorbing them into its body. The others began attacking it, but chipping away at the mass of bones and armor didn't slow the golem down.

I picked up my spear and shield just as the surrounding dwarves divided to reveal Dirk across the room. I ran at him. He raised his hand, summoning a spear and launched it at me. It was a powerful throw, but it burst into light when it made contact with my shield. I began picking up speed, charging at him to attack. He threw another spear, but I deflected it away. Within striking distance, I lunged, but Dirk was able to summon his bladed staff in time to push my spear off target. I followed the attack with a shield bash, catching his jaw with its edge. The blow caused him to stumble, and I speared his lower back. Both our weapons dissipated, and through the pain, he telekinetically pushed me away.

Dirk moved in to attack again. He shot arrows of energy from his hands that I blocked with the ethereal shield that I still carried. He then summoned another glaive and swung it down at my shoulder. I raised my shield in time to block it, but he used the other end to sweep my legs out from under me. I fell hard on my back, and my shield returned to the magical realm from which I summoned it. Dirk spun his staff around to impale me, but my golem stepped forward, kicking him across the room into one of the many obsidian columns that supported the chamber.

The bone golem had nearly doubled in size from absorbing all the undead dwarves that it attacked. Its head was nearing the high ceiling, but there weren't many dwarves left for it to absorb.

While fighting off the last of the reanimated dwarves, I doubled-kicked one in the face. "It smells like defeat, doesn't it? With a capital FEET!" I told the fallen dwarf before it was absorbed into the mighty bone golem.

"There's my boys," I said, spotting my obsidian swords across the large room. I telekinetically pulled them to my hands and cautiously approached Dirk's body lying at the base of the magma-filled column that he was kicked into. Blood oozed from the corner of his mouth, and I could tell that he suffered many broken bones. He was unconscious while his blood worked to heal him, but I knew he would awaken soon. I plunged both swords into his chest and watched as his body shriveled to a leathery husk.

CHAPTER XII

AMBROS VS BYRON

"BYRON IS BEYOND THOSE DOORS, MASTER," Bones' voice boomed. "I CAN FEEL HIS SORCEROUS PRESENCE."

Looking away from Dirk's corpse, I saw the door at the far end of the chamber between rows of columns. "Then let's say hello."

"BUT I'M TOO BIG. YOU'LL HAVE TO GO ALONE."

The heavy iron doors leading into the next room appeared large to me, but were tiny compared to the monstrosity that I had created. A wheel attached to a pulley system next to the doors allowed me to open them, and I stepped into another large room.

There was a large fountain of volcanic magma at the center of the room. An enormous, iron statue of a heavily armored dwarf stood proudly atop an obsidian pillar where molten rock poured into a hot pool. A hole in the high ceiling allowed heat to vent from the chamber.

Byron walked out slowly from behind the fountain with his hands clasped together. The ancient necromancer, in my father's body, wore a regal green and black suit with a black cape. He opened his arms to me, and for the length of a single breath, I wanted to run to him. Memories came back to me of pop splitting bones on the porch while I scrapped out marrow. I remembered all those early mornings when we walked through Ashwood to collect mushrooms to make bread.

"My son," he said in a soothing voice, drawing me from my thoughts. "I am so proud of you. You have come far and traveled a difficult road. I know you have many questions. Come with me. We can find the answers together."

I felt his will pressing upon me, reminding me that he is not my pop. I stepped up to look straight into his eyes. "You're Byron, created by Shadowrath himself, and tasked with resurrecting him, should he fall. I am not your son!"

"Oh, but you are," he argued. "I healed your wounds and granted you eternal life. The blood which flows through your veins is my gift to you, my son." He reached out and placed a hand on my shoulder. "Together, you and I can free Magnus from this magical prison and destroy the dragon race forever!"

Remembering Lorena's sword piercing that shoulder and destroying my arm, I broke free from his influence. My pupils dilated, and my fingers clenched into a fist as it came up under his chin. A spike of ethereal energy stuck through his skull, breaking through the top!

"I am not your son!" I yelled in his twitching, misshapen face. "You brought war to my city! You killed my friend! You used me in your experiments! You will not manipulate me!"

Lightning popped and crackled up my arm to strike my enemy. It arced from the tip of the ethereal spike and struck the rocky ceiling high above. He breathed an unsettling, guttural sound before his eyes exploded and his head caught fire. I retracted the spike, and pushed his stinking corpse away from me. As soon as he struck the floor, he vanished.

"Son of a lich! It was an illusion! Ambros, you ass!" I scolded myself, realizing I had been deceived. I gasped and turned quickly, expecting the real Byron to attack from behind, but no one was there.

Byron's familiar voice thundered from the dwarf statue. "You may hold power over the dead, but do you wield it over death itself?"

The metal that made up the large, iron statue scraped and squealed as it came to life.

"Shit!" I cursed. Looking up at the metal monstrosity, I unsheathed my swords and readied myself. "I'm going to need some help in here, Bones!" I yelled back to him in the other room.

Bones pounded his fists against the thick wall over the door, but he could not break it. He began dismantling himself, so he could fit through the door and reassemble himself inside the room.

The iron golem leaped from the column that it stood upon, punching down at me. I was able to dodge the devastating attack, but I lost my footing and fell. The immense force sent cracks snaking across the stone floor. It extended a hand and launched a spear from its palm that pierced my thigh. I yelled out in pain and noticed there was a chain that linked the spear to the golem's hand.

"Uh, this isn't going well," I commented before I was yanked up from the floor and swung around over the golem's head.

I lost my grip on Scourge and Devour, so they were thrown somewhere across the room. I felt the contents of my stomach rise up into my throat, and blood I had drank from the castle architect spewed from my mouth. I was then slammed onto the ground. "Oh, my face!" I grunted.

The golem retracted the chain, dragging me across the floor and pulling me into its sharp hand. I felt the spear rip from my leg, tearing the muscle. I was being squeezed to the point I thought my body would burst when I saw Bones rise up from behind the golem and strike it with both fists, causing it to stumble and drop me.

While the golem was down on its hands and knees, Bones struck it again. It fell flat on the floor, cracking more stones.

Byron rose out of a shadow cast along the floor by the two golems and walked toward me, seemingly uninterested in the monumental battle happening next to him.

I reached for my swords before remembering I had lost them.

He raised a hand and lightening arced from his fingertips. The lightening raced toward me, but I summoned two swords from the ethereal realm. I caught the bolt of electricity at the tip of one sword and allowed it to pass harmlessly through my body before expelling it from the other sword back to Byron.

Before it could strike him, he dropped back into the shadow on the floor. A hand suddenly clasped over my mouth, an arm reached around me, and I felt my body go weightless as I was dragged down into the floor. I fought against him, pulling free within the strange dimension to find myself standing on the opposite side of the stone floor. Everything was transparent, appearing to have no mass. Below me, on the other side of the floor, I could see the two mighty golems still battling.

Byron's eyes were shut as if concentrating deeply, and dark spirits took shape around him. I was suddenly restrained by spirits manifesting behind me while others seemed to reach inside me, taking the shape of friends and loved ones who've passed on. I screamed out in pain, but it wasn't a physical pain; it was one that tore into my very soul, conjuring up intense feelings of loss, heartbreak, and helplessness.

I released a pulse of energy that pushed them away from me. I swung my ethereal swords, which appeared solid in this realm, destroying those that I cut. I fought harder and faster as I made my way to Byron, tearing through the many wraiths he continued to summon. His eyes were still shut, but he no doubt knew what was happening around him. When I finally came within reach of him and swung my swords, he effortlessly caught both blades in his hands. His eyes popped open, and I was thrown back into the real world above.

Byron stood looking down from the large, obsidian column in the center of the lava fountain. "It's foolish to believe one could kill me," he said. "Even I don't know how to die, and believe me, I've tried innumerable times."

I called upon a quick spell to protect myself from heat and told him, "Then you must not have tried hard enough."

Summoning dual swords, I leaped up to the searing hot column and swung them simultaneously only to be halted by a staff that magically formed in Byron's hand.

"HAGH! HAGH! HAGH!" he laughed cruelly while the two golems fought around us.

He spun the staff and struck my swords with enough force that they returned to the netherworld. I quickly created a shield to block his next attack, but it, too, was immediately destroyed. With each weapon I summoned, Byron knocked it away. I kicked him in the groin and forced him away from me.

He dropped to his knees for only a moment before raising his hands, bringing the lava from the fountain up around us. The large fist of the iron golem passed through the fire, splashing lava over us. My fire resistance spell protected me from being blistered.

Byron then sent lava from the wall to swirl around me and wear away at my resistance, but I pushed the heat of the lava way, causing it to solidify. He telekinetically pushed me through the frozen ore into the battling golems, and I had to move quickly to keep from being squashed beneath their feet as they punched and grappled one another.

The iron golem struck Bones with a fist covered in burning lava. A chunk from his shoulder burst loose and fell nearby. The bodies that made up the shoulder hurried back to the golem and was absorbed into the mass. Bones caught the iron golem's next attack and threw him to the ground.

The floor could no longer bear the colossal weight. It split and caved in, causing all of us to slide into a deep crevasse. Byron and I were last to slip into the fissure, so we were above the golems as we fell.

The lava that had been flowing into the fountain poured into the hole from various passages, casting an abysmal light on the wall of rock that surrounded us as we fell deeper into the earth. The two golems broke away large portions of stone during their decent, widening the crevasse.

Byron dropped onto a large stone that had broken loose, and he launched a barrage of energy bolts up at me. The thin, white missiles sped toward me, but I created an energy shield while I fell through the earth. The magic missiles exploded on contact with the barrier.

Byron sent a shockwave through the stone he was on, obliterating it to dust. I was temporarily blinded as I passed through it, so I didn't notice the wily necromancer slipping by to be above me during our descent.

A crushing energy field enveloped me, and lightning arced to me from its spherical surface. My extremities pulled and contorted with the flow of electricity, charring my skin in its wake. I felt pain, but I knew it was only temporary and that the blood which now flowed through my veins was already working to repair the damage.

I couldn't see much of what was happening beyond the energy field, but I knew I was still falling. My mind reached for the arcing bolts of electricity until they were caught, and I pushed them away. They pierced the barrier and broke the spell that held me. The electricity popped across the rock walls, stirring up more rock and debris that put Byron on the defensive.

Far below us, beyond the battling golems, I began to see light. Whether the bottom was liquid or solid, I knew I wasn't going to like the impact, so I commanded Bones to "Divide!"

"YES, MASTER!"

The magical bond that held the dead soldiers together broke to allow them to act independently. The massive golem appeared to crumble as the hundreds of skeletons, zombie dwarves and goblins began separating. As they disconnected, I issued another command to take hold of each other. The undead army's decent slowed, distancing them from the iron golem that fell ahead, and the detached dead took hold of those nearest to them to form a large net. Those around the edge of the undead web plunged swords into the rock to stop their decent.

I fell into the net and looked up to see large rocks raining down. The skeletons and zombies that filled the chasm opened and shut holes in their net to allow the rocks to pass through until Byron reached them. Pointing their weapons upward, they created a deadly trap of blades for him to land in, but Byron avoided it by halting his fall.

I struggled to stand on the uneven surface of bones and armor to look up at him. "Why are you doing this? What do you want from me?"

While holding his position above me, he answered, "I want a younger, more perfect vessel, so I need to know your limitations if I'm going to transfer my mind into your body." His green robes flowed in the hot air that blew up from the deep. "And I will no longer be affected by time. I will unlock the secrets of the undead and grow beyond your need for blood, beyond your need for darkness. I will be truly immortal and god over all life."

"Your desire for power and control makes you no different from dragons."

"Oh, but you lack the vision to see the difference."

"Enlighten me," I asked of him.

"Very well."

Byron formed a ball of black fire within his hands and launched it at me. I sprang away from the blast, but it began burning away the undead like dried leaves.

"NO!" I yelled, but there was nothing I could do to stop it. I fell through the disintegrating web of bones, and the green light that held them together burned out. Above me, I could see the last of my army turn to dust.

"I'll be down here, waiting for you," I told Byron through a hard smile as I fell.

Down, down I fell toward the center of the Earth. The iron golem had fallen out of sight but left a gaping crevasse to pass through. It finally opened into an immense cavern illuminated by a lake of molten rock. Not far away, I could see the shoreline, so I guided my fall and slowed my descent to land on the course, black sand.

A hot wind blew from the beautiful red waters, and I remembered being out on the ocean with Lorena. She was gone now. Perhaps she was sailing again with her friend in the afterlife she had believed in. But Pop and Jinxie were still dead, and I desperately needed them back. I looked down at my hands as I opened and closed them. "I need to get back to Ashwood," I reminded myself.

Thunder cracked, and I shielded my eyes from the flash of light. A bolt of lightning struck the sand nearby, leaving Byron on the black shore.

"Where the dragons rule to control their food supply, I will rule to give all life purpose," he began to explain, walking toward me.

"And what purpose is that?"

"Building my empire."

"Life needs the freedom to choose how to live," I argued. "You can't crown yourself king and expect everyone to remain happy under your rule forever."

"That's exactly what I expect. My world will be made perfect!" he shouted, rising slowly above the sand to look down on me. "And no one will have the power to overthrow me, nor corrupt my kingdom," he added, raising his hands.

"Only you will be the corruptor," I corrected him. "You must live among your people as one of them and be an example for them to strive for."

The wind changed directions, pulling back to sea. It swirled and drew funnels of magma up to create boiling storms on the red lake. Four magma cyclones headed to shore.

"Just because you look like my father doesn't mean I won't kill you," I yelled at him over the roar of the approaching storms.

"HAGH! This body simply acts as a focal point for my power in the physical realm. You can't destroy me."

The cyclones reached shore and stirred up sand,

making it impossible to see more than a few feet. As the cyclones moved closer together, red lightning arced between them and began striking me. The protection from fire spell that I had cast earlier was eroded away, and the swirling lava closed in around me. The four cyclones merged as one, and I stood at its core as the intense heat burned away my hair and scorched my skin.

I levitated and pulled my extremities in close to my body. Focusing my thoughts, I pushed the searing heat of the lava away while I absorbed multiple lightning strikes. I then released a powerful pulse of electrical energy that destroyed the magma cyclone.

I saw the molten ore splash over a protective barrier that Byron had conjured. "Impressive," he commented.

My entire body felt raw. I looked down at myself for a moment to see black sand clinging to a charred, naked body.

Byron began concentrating intently, but I didn't wait for him to cast whatever spell he was conjuring. I whipped him with a powerful bolt of lightning. The white, jagged light reached from my hand to entangle him. I lifted him up and slammed him on the ground. Before attempting to get up, he pointed at me, and through gritted teeth, he threw me back several yards.

"You are a clever sorcerer, much like your father," Byron hissed, getting to his feet. He extended a hand toward the lake, causing the lava to give birth to an enormous dragon composed of molten earth.

"Now that's one big dragon," I commented.

I then noticed ashes falling down around us. It was the remains of my army Byron disintegrated. They had floated down from high above to settle on the beach.

I suddenly realized that the soil and sand that covered the earth wasn't just eroded stone, but it was also the decomposed remains of all that once lived. It was life broken down to its basic elements.

I clenched my fingers and raised my fists. I fell to my knees upon the black sand, and with all the power within me, I called for the dead. "RISE!"

Particles of sand clumped together all around us to form the skeletons and bodies of not just people but of giants and even dragons that had died long ago.

Byron levitated several feet into the air to escape the charging dead. He launched bolts of energy, causing his targets to explode.

The magma dragon passed over us, breathing fire. The extreme heat turned many of my black sand soldiers into glass.

Byron quickly raised a rigid hand, causing an area of black sand to solidify into a long spike and jut toward me. My unnatural reflexes allowed me to dodge the six foot spike. I ran across the beach toward him, calling a spear from the ethereal realm to my hands. Byron continued creating spikes, impaling my summoned warriors, but I avoided them all as I traced a large circle in the sand with my spear. I then leaped into the air to kill the ancient necromancer.

"You've come far enough," he said, holding me in midair. He pulled his fists in near his chest, and his body glowed a bright white. He pushed his hands out and the light exploded from him across the beach to turn my army to glass. "I've already told you, you cannot destroy me. Even if you separate my head from my body, I will…"

A dragon under my command came up from

beneath the black sand beach and swallowed the ancient necromancer. The great beast disappeared back into the sand.

"I know," I said to the space in front of me where Byron once levitated. "I just wanted to bring you discomfort."

The dragon he had called for immediately lost its form and splashed across the beach, far from where I was standing.

"Well, I wasn't going to ride you out of here, anyway!" I yelled, picking up and throwing a severed glass foot. "Perhaps I should do something about this skin before trying to find my way out."

I closed my eyes and blocked out the sound of the churning lake. I focused on my heartbeat as it pumped unnatural blood through my veins. I willed more blood to the surface where it could heal my charred skin quicker. Within just a few beats, I was back to normal. I had skin and a fresh set of clothing.

Where the magma dragon fell, I could see a doorway carved into the black stone wall.

"I don't want to go that way," I said aloud to myself. I looked up into the darkness for the crevasse I had fallen through, but I couldn't see it. "Perhaps I can pass through rock like Byron did when he pulled me into the floor. I read his journal. I should be able to do it."

I closed my eyes and clinched my fists. My muscles drew tighter and tighter. The tension suddenly released, and I opened my eyes again to that strange dimension. I felt no heat from the nearby lake of lava. I stood on the black sand beach, but I couldn't feel the tiny particles beneath my feet. I could see the physical world, but I didn't seem to be a part of it. Looking down,

I could see Byron far below me. He launched bolts of energy only to have them reflected back on himself from the walls of his dragon prison that I captured him in.

"Run while you can," I heard him say as though nothing lay between us. "You can't hide from me. I will find you. I will find you!"

"I won't play hard to get. When you're ready, come see me. Oh, and don't be surprised when you don't find Hela waiting up for you; she's dead."

"What? You lie!"

"I'm sorry," I apologized sincerely. "I know all too well that losing those we love is worse than death."

"No!" he cried. "NO!"

I looked up and willed myself through the volcano to the dwarven ruins above while Byron's screams faded into the darkness below.

CHAPTER XIII

THE CHEST IS OPENED

Through the transparent world around me, my sharp, vampire vision spotted two people sitting in the distance. One of them appeared to be waving to get my attention, but that couldn't be because I was many levels beneath them. I passed through walls of stone like an apparition to reach a sloping passage where the couple sat.

"Ambros," a dark-skinned woman said before I materialized.

I felt the weight of my body again as I anchored myself back into the physical world.

"It's so good to see you," the woman said, standing to hug me. "My name is Vistilia, and you've already met Manius."

That's when I finally noticed who the other person was in the wide passageway. A flood of memories and feelings washed over me.

"It looks like you've grown up," Manius said.

"Not quite enough, it seems; you're still taller," I laughed and shook his hand, but he pulled me close for a hug.

"How've you been?" Manius asked, sitting down again on a rock and leaning back against the wall of the dimly lit tunnel.

I chuckled and raised my hands, answering sarcastically, "Fantastic!"

I then felt a familiar sensation and looked up and down the long, sloping tunnel. It was suspiciously clear except for the three of us and the rock that Manius sat upon. I suddenly realized it wasn't just any old rock. It was a carved chunk of black obsidian.

I pointed to it and asked, "What is that you're sitting on?"

A grin cracked his face that confirmed my suspicion, and I, too, smiled.

"May I see her?" I asked politely.

Manius stood from the chest. He picked it up and sat it at my feet. I kneeled next to it and rubbed my hands over its cold surface, feeling the carved handles on its sides. I was about to lift the lid when Manius spoke.

"Ambrosius still lives."

I stopped what I was doing and looked up at him.

He nodded his head. "He has been nudging me in the right direction all these years."

"How? How is he communicating to you?"

"That night in Ashwood, he drank a special elixir that allowed his consciousness to pass on to me through the drinking of his blood."

"Can he hear me right now?"

"I don't know. He doesn't speak to me often, but I know he is with me."

"Why didn't you tell me this before leaving Ashwood with his corpse over your shoulder?" I asked angrily.

"Ambrosius told us both what we needed to know," he answered sharply.

"Why did you give him to Byron?" I spat.

"I needed his help fighting the giants, and I had nothing else that he wanted."

I was about to yell again when I caught myself; I didn't like the feeling of anger swelling within me. I took a deep breath to calm myself. Moving on, I said, "I read what happened to Eve in Byron's journal."

Vistilia walked over and hugged me.

"I'm sorry," Manius finally said, wiping his eyes.

"So why are you still down here?" I asked to change the subject.

While keeping his eyes on me, Manius extended his arm, and his fist struck a magical barrier. He then leaned against it.

I walked over to the invisible barrier but was not blocked by it. I was able to pass through it unhindered like the one I stepped through earlier.

"Until the spell is broken, I am trapped down here. I sent word to Dirk and Byron that I had found Arethil's remains and that I would send a group of dwarves to deliver the chest to them. Dirk warned me of Byron's true motives, so I had the dwarves hide the chest before Byron came in search of it. I reclaimed it when a zombie goblin found it and began dragging it back to his master."

I laughed. "That was one of my goblins. I sent several in search of the chest while I fought Byron's army."

"Did you kill him?" Manius asked nervously.

Rubbing my chin, I answered, "I believe Dirk may have killed that one."

Confused, he clarified, "No, I mean Byron. Did you kill Byron?"

"Oh, no. He can't be killed, but I did lock him in a temporary prison."

Manius exhaled a sigh of relief. "Good; I still need him to break this spell," he explained, tapping his fist against the barrier. "But I can't let him get his hands on this chest."

I nodded in agreement.

"So you must be the one to take it to the surface," he told me.

"What will happen?"

"I don't know, but legend says that sunlight will resurrect the phoenix where moonlight will awaken the dragon."

"I am quite familiar with the legend, and it also says that Shadowrath and Arethil remain in an eternal struggle within the dark dimension. We can't release one expecting the other to remain imprisoned," I argued.

Manius thought on it for a moment, pacing the floor. "Ambrosius has led me this far. I must have faith that releasing Arethil is for the best."

"I wish I could speak to him."

Manius put a hand on my shoulder. "I know you do, son. I know you do."

For a moment, I thought Pop was speaking through Manius, but it may have just been his choice of words.

"Well, I should probably get going. I don't imagine that prison will hold Byron for very long," I said, stepping over to the chest. "How heavy is this thing, anyway?"

"You shouldn't have any trouble; vampires are unnaturally strong."

I took hold of the carved handles of the chest and lifted it with ease. I stepped beyond the magical barrier, and looking back, I asked Vistilia, "Are you a prisoner, too."

She took hold of his hand before answering, "I enjoy his company."

"I hope you two are not stuck down here for much longer," I told them.

Vistilia shook her head. "We won't be."

I turned and began following the long tunnel to the surface. There were no torches to light my way, but I had no trouble seeing through the darkness. I walked for what seemed like hours, carrying the obsidian chest, but I didn't tire. It was so quiet that I could hear the slow, rhythmic beat of my heart and the rush of blood in my ears. To break the silence, I began talking aloud.

"If I can feel your presence through the walls of this chest, perhaps my voice can permeate it. My name is Ambros, and I am from a Dark Elf city called Ashwood. And no, I didn't say ass wood," I laughed.

I heard nothing from the chest, but that didn't stop me from talking. I told Arethil everything about myself and all that I had learned on my long journey. I reached the end of the tunnel, but, before stepping out into the sun, I sat the obsidian chest down to pull a hood up over my head and cover my hands with gloves. I carried the chest out onto a hillside, and I took a deep breath of fresh air. On a distant mountainside, I could see the castle where I had entered the dwarven ruins.

I placed the chest on the grassy slope and lifted the lid. Sunlight illuminated the interior of the black obsidian chest and ancient runes became visible along its surface. A fume of smoke rose from the ashes inside, and a fire roared from the center. I fell back from the chest, my eyebrows singed from the heat.

A tiny ball of fire rose from the chest, pulsating like a beating heart. Dust and bones followed and took the shape of a bird around the fire. Extending its skeletal wings, it was eight feet from tip to tip. Burning tendrils grew from its fiery heart, extending throughout its body with every beat. Fire engulfed the skeleton, and I shielded my eyes from the brightness. When the light dimmed, I saw a magnificent bird floating before me. The fire that once burned had become feathers that shifted between red, yellow, and white hues. I kneeled and bowed my head to the great phoenix, feeling a radiance of warmth from her.

"Arethil."

"*There is no need to bow before me, dear Ambros,*" the phoenix said to my mind. Its voice was soft and feminine. "*I did not come to be worshipped. I came to create and live as one of you.*"

Fire, once again, burned outward from her chest, transforming her from a colorful bird to a beautiful elf wearing white and gold clothing. She was as tall as a Light Elf. Her skin seemed to glow from a warm light within. Her hair shimmered in the sunlight, shifting in color like the feathers that had just covered her body, and her eyes were a brilliant gold.

"I do not have much time," she said vocally, looking at the open chest on the ground next to her. "My absence will soon be realized, and the dragon will call for his servant."

"I have many questions."

She nodded that she knew. "You will find the answers to those questions through the drinking of my blood."

The word itself awakened the dark hunger within me, and I lusted after it. I stood still, resisting it, savoring the anticipation.

"My blood will burn you, but I will not let it destroy you." She turned her head to the side. "Now come, vampire. Take the answers you seek."

A slit opened across her neck, and hot, steaming blood oozed forth. I was on her before I even realized I had moved, my arms and legs wrapped tightly around her, constricting like a snake. She stood still, unmoved by my weight. I felt her godly blood burn away my lips and scorch my tongue as I drank it in.

Through her blood, I saw an ancient star that developed a consciousness over billions of years. The star reached the end of its long life and collapsed upon itself, solidifying into a dense stone. It cracked open, allowing the mind to separate itself from the remains.

The tiny star wandered the universe in search of others like it but found no one. In response to the loneliness, the sentient star developed multiple personalities and soon divided into eight separate entities.

Throughout the cosmos, they collected many different elements. They found that a simple combination of them could create life, so they set out to seed planets. Eons later, they returned. To their surprise, not only did life perpetuate, but, on some worlds, it evolved into intelligent life! This was one such world.

The planet had become home to a multitude of organisms, a lush oasis within the cosmic sea. The eight tiny stars circled the world to observe its many inhabitants and soon discovered a beautiful, fiercely intelligent race called elves. The stars took the form of birds to study them closer, but the elves could sense great power emanating from them. They began painting pictures of them and leaving offerings of food and flowers at sunrise and sunset.

After many years, seven of the stars left to visit other seeded worlds. One stayed behind to reveal itself to the elves and live among them. It transformed itself into a beautiful elf and chose the name Arethil.

Little did they know that deep within the earth a terrible race was evolving. Before the elves, giant reptiles ruled the planet. Many preferred living underground and in the oceans. Over the millennia, they grew immensely powerful. While their cousins went extinct on the surface, the intelligent dragons thrived in the underworld until their numbers grew too great. After much fighting, they began exploring the world above. It was only a matter of time before they encountered the equally intelligent but peaceful race of elves. But if they would not bow to their dragon overlords, they would be destroyed!

As the dragons brought death and destruction across the land, one elf stepped forward with a plan to end the war and bring balance back to the world— Ambrosius.

Through Arethil's blood, I saw billions of years

in mere seconds. Unable to drink more, I released my grip on her and collapsed to my hands and knees, overwhelmed by the visions.

I took a few deep breaths before speaking. "What must I do?" I asked, looking down at the blades of grass between my fingers.

"Simple," she began to answer, reaching down to lift my chin. "Live."

I stood up, confused by her answer.

To dispel my confusion, she added, "While you live, I know you will do everything that you should do."

"But what about Shadowrath? Won't he escape now that you're free?" I asked fearfully.

"I cannot stay," Arethil said, shaking her head. "For that very reason, I must return to the void."

"Can you destroy him, perhaps with the help of the other phoenixes?" I suggested.

"I know that I cannot do it on my own, but I cannot leave to find them."

"So you're stuck here," I stated solemnly. "What about Byron? He will not stop until he has the chest. But he does not wish to free Shadowrath; he wants to take his and your power for himself."

"The physical aspect of Shadowrath's form may have been destroyed, but his strength has not diminished. He created Byron, for he feared he would one day require a new vessel to contain his immense power. If Byron thinks he can fool his dark master, he is mistaken. It is the lure of power that controls him."

Pointing to the lovely form she took, I said, "But you can heal yourself."

"Yes. I can produce my own physical form when needed, but I cannot take it into the void."

"That is why your bones were left behind in the chest," I understood.

Looking up at the bright blue sky, she took a deep breath. "I must return to my prison, now," she announced and turned to the chest.

"Wait!" I held my hand out to stop her. "Arethil, I don't want to do this alone," I told her sadly. "Can you bring Pop back from the dead? Can you bring my beloved Jinxie back from ash? Can you help me?"

Arethil smiled warmly and placed a comforting hand on my shoulder. "I have given you all that you need to continue your journey."

Asking no more of her, I bowed to bid her farewell. "Thank you, great phoenix."

"Ambros," she said caringly. "I know you feel your wish far exceeds your grasp, but you are much closer than you realize."

I nodded and smiled, for her uplifting words eased the stress weighing heavily on me. She kissed my forehead before transforming from elf to bird, and she disappeared into the chest, the lid slamming shut behind her. I peeked into the chest to find it as before—filled with the bones of a bird.

Sitting in the grass for a long while, I decided on what I should do. I needed to find a safe place to leave the chest. "Safe. Safe," I repeated before settling on an answer.

CHAPTER XIV

RETURN TO ASHWOOD

I still had a lot to do and a lot of traveling ahead, so I began by following my keen sense of death to a graveyard. I sat the obsidian chest down at the edge of the area before walking among the graves.

"This is no human graveyard," I said to myself as I looked over the many moss-covered mounds. "Well, whatever's buried here, I could use some help."

Concentrating on my hand, a slit opened across the palm allowing blood to ooze out. I pressed my hand into the moss covering one of the graves, letting the blood seep down to the body within. I felt movement. The earth shifted, breaking the smooth layer of moss. I took a step back, clutching my hand to help the dark blood heal the flesh quicker.

Stones that covered the body were pushed aside, and a half-human creature pulled itself free from its grave. Standing over head high, it was the remains of a centaur.

"Oh, it's one of you. What's your name?"

In my mind, I heard a series of snorts and grunts. I tried mimicking the sounds, but the centaur only shook his head that I wasn't pronouncing it right. After five attempts to say his name, I gave up.

"Ah, forget it! Your name will be Horse-Man. No. That's no good. Man-Horse, um.... Horsem! Your name is Horsem. Now, pick up that chest, Horsem, and let's get out of here."

The skeletal centaur plodded over and lifted the chest. I summoned a thick layer of furs to cover his boney back and ribs for me to sit upon before starting the long journey back to Ashwood.

Missing my swords, I thought about how I could recreate their effect. "Pop imbued my obsidian swords with power. I don't see why I couldn't do the same with ethereal weapons. I don't know where to begin with causing madness. Perhaps I should start with Devour," I said to myself.

So while traveling to my old homeland, I worked to create an ethereal sword with the same magical effect as Devour. I trapped animals to test my weapons on, but I couldn't recreate the same effect. Adding fire only cauterized the wounds I inflicted.

After a few weeks of slow traveling and unsuccessful attempts, I reached my old homeland. I strapped the chest to Horsem's back and covered it with furs. I led him to the obsidian door of the city where Torvin and the other elf hunters met me.

"It is good to see you alive, young Ambros," Torvin said. "Every time you leave, we're afraid you'll never return."

I responded with only an understanding nod.

He placed his hand on the door carved to look like elves, and the two halves stepped aside, revealing the passage through the mountain to the city.

"Would you like us to watch over your, uh…"

"He's a centaur, and he stays with me."

"Yes, my lord," Torvin bowed, and the other hunters followed his example.

I raised a hand to stop them. "Please, that's unnecessary. I'm not my father. I'm not the guardian of Ashwood."

"We would prefer one of our own over a serpent as guardian," Torvin whispered.

"I know, old friend. I know." I patted his shoulder and led Horsem into the mountain. The stale air of the tunnel changed to that familiar earthy aroma just before reaching the city inside. Outside, there were still a couple hours more of daylight, but inside, night had already fallen.

The city had suffered minor damage from the war Byron had brought. Many elves still worked to make repairs.

I stopped outside Yndra's black tower. I pointed at Horsem and then to the spot where he stood, telling him to stay put. I shut my eyes and entered the spirit world. I then passed through the tower door. The large obsidian egg that was broken had been cleaned up and another egg had replaced it.

I needed to kill Yndra, so the Dark Elves of Ashwood could appoint their own leader. I could then take Jinxic's ashes with me to study in Magesticc.

I floated across the room and up the stairs to the

second floor to find Yndra standing by a long table with her back to me. Her pointed, black tail swayed calmly from side to side. It protruded from an opening in the back of her crimson dress that complimented her shapely figure.

This was it. This was my chance. I quietly floated up behind her. I could see that she was looking over drawings of the obsidian egg and notes of its construction in a book. The ashes I had given her were in a jar nearby. Various instruments used to study the ashes littered the table.

I didn't need to waste any more time. I returned to my physical form, and an ethereal dagger took shape in my hand. I raised it to slay the Black Dragon.

"I know you've come for more than just your beloved's remains," the dragon's words caught me by surprise. "If you should kill me, the World Council will only send another dragon to govern Ashwood, and one even more sinister than myself." I could hear her smiling through her voice. "The only difference being, I mean to destroy the dragons, whereas they mean to destroy the elves."

I lowered my dagger, allowing it to dissipate. "How did you know I was here?" I asked curiously, thinking I was undetectable.

She turned to me, smiling. "I hear more than just footsteps," she admitted, knocking on her chest. "Not to mention…" She chuckled and tapped her nose.

Closing my fingers into a fist, I scolded myself through gritted teeth, "Smell!"

She walked by me to open her new obsidian egg. "I love it here in Ashwood," she continued. "The council believes I am loyal to them, but I can work in secret here where I could not at the palace."

"So you really mean to kill your own kind?" I asked, picking up a jar containing Jinxie's ashes.

"With only a few copies of myself, I can overthrow the World Council, shifting the balance of power to the elves. With their help, we can track down the great dragon dens and sever their bloodlines, ensuring they go extinct. We may be strong, but our numbers are fewer than most realize."

"And what if you fail to kill the council leaders?"

"Then it will be no different if you killed me now," she answered. "At least by letting me live, there's a chance my plan will work," she added.

"Where is the other Yndra?" I asked, looking around.

"She tried to save you and your charismatic cohort, but Byron's pet vampire mortally wounded her."

"Was she the copy, or are you?" Realizing the rudeness of my question, I quickly asked another to cover it. "I mean, how do you feel?"

Yndra took an emotional breath and covered her mouth, turning away. "It's like... It's like I myself died," she stammered.

"I'm sorry," I apologized for both her loss and the pain I stirred within her, remembering my own loss.

"Our minds were linked. They worked as one, doubling my intellect," she continued with her back to me. "When I found your father's notes, I began to devise a terrible plan to assassinate the council members so that I could rule. But once I had two minds working together, I saw a better world and the path to reach it. My emotions were also broadened. What she felt, I felt. So when she died, I felt myself die." She turned to look at me with tears falling down her cheek. "It seems we've both lost someone very dear to us." And then she gasped, realizing I was alone. "Where is Miss Eleanor?"

"She didn't make it," I answered sadly.

"I am so sorry to hear that," she sighed. "She was a lovely human."

I pinched the palm of my hand and pulled a cloth pouch into existence to empty the jar of ashes into. Clearly, she hadn't made any progress.

Yndra ran her fingers between her black horns, through her raven hair. "I did all I know to do. I found nothing but common minerals. Not even Ambrosius' elixir is potent enough to recreate life from it. I'm sorry I could not do more."

"You've done plenty," I told her, tying the pouch to my belt. "I've been going about it the wrong way. Thank you."

She placed a hand on my shoulder. "Now that you're home, we could work together to solve this."

I shook my head and was about to tell her that I had no plans of staying, but she interrupted.

"Imagine what we will accomplish with both our minds and the network of minds we create. We will change the world," she declared proudly.

I took a moment to think. It seemed she was doing the best thing she could do, but it didn't feel right for me. I finally told her what Pop told me, "I'm sorry, but my journey lies along a different path."

Taking hold of my hand, she pleaded with sad eyes, "But I need your help. You must stay. Your kin needs your help."

"Goodbye, Yndra. I wish you luck on your

quest."

"But you must. You must stay," she repeated.

Pulling free of her hand, I was about to leave when sharp fingers tightened around my neck!

"I wasn't asking," she clarified, her sadness turning to enjoyment. "I know that you are different; I can hear the drumming of your heart. It drums the same beat as the girl vampire, Takara."

She lifted me off the floor and pulled me close. Her nostrils flared as she smelled my breath. "You did what I had planned to do with that elf girl—you took her immortal blood for yourself!"

"No," I struggled to say within her grip.

"Shhh," she hissed. "I'll make this quick."

Sensing what she was about to do, I quickly directed a telekinetic shield to my back just as she slammed me against the floor. Had I not, I would have been smashed into paste.

"Stay out of my head!" she yelled, throwing me into the wall.

"You had me fooled," I coughed, shaking a finger at her. "I believed every lie you fed me. I was about to leave, allowing you to live."

Her heels clacked as she walked slowly across the stone floor to me. "Oh, I still plan to destroy the dragons, but will you help me or no? Will you give me enough of your blood to duplicate it, or will I have to take it?"

"I can't trust you to live forever."

I raised my hand, but she lunged. Her black wings unfurled. She caught my hand and gripped my face in her dark talons.

"Your sacrifice for your people will be remembered for eternity," she whispered.

Struggling to speak within her grasp, I asked, "Why can't I live for eternity and tell them of your sacrifice instead?"

Yndra broke into laughter. "No, I think I'll hang your decapitated corpse over the obsidian egg and drain every last drop of your immortal blood into it."

"What happened to saving the elves?" I laughed to dispel my fear. "I'm an elf."

"But you're a vampire, now, Ambros," she answered excitedly. "They will not trust you to live among them."

Yndra's sharp thumbnail pierced the skin of my palm. Blood oozed from the wound and trickled down my arm. Her forked, black tongue touched it and followed the stream to my hand.

"Mmmm, I just love the taste of blood, don't you?"

I sent a silent command to my hand where an ethereal blade jutted from my palm, entered the dragon lady's mouth, and protruded out the back of her head. The blood from my hand added an unexpected vampiric effect to the blade which quickly drew all of her blood into the ethereal plane. Her supple, black skin shriveled and cracked.

"Oooo! It does wonders for the skin. I'll take it!" I yelled, thinking the effect was similar enough to Devour.

I retracted the blade, and the body immediately began growing to its original size.

"Oh, not this again!"

I ran for the stairs, but the quickly expanding body pushed me toward the center of the room against the edge of the obsidian egg where I tipped over into it. I slid down to the bottom of the hollowed out crystal sphere, and the top fell, slamming into place. I could only see a growing darkness through the smooth walls until the weight of the dragon forced it through the hole in the floor that it rested in. The egg fell to the stone floor of the level beneath it and broke apart. Looking up, I could see the ceiling and the walls of the tower cracking under the pressure of Yndra's enormity. I ran outside and a safe distance away as the obsidian tower collapsed in on itself, causing tremors throughout the entire city.

Elves and fairies hurried from their homes to see what had happened.

Magma oozed up to the surface, encircling the remains of the tower as it slowly sank into the earth.

Looking to one of the elves standing next to me, I said to him, "That dragon lady could sure fill out a dress. Wooo!" I blew. "But damn, she turned out to be one fat bitch."

"Is she dead?" I heard someone ask.

"Oh, I'm sure of it," I answered with a chuckle.

"What should we do?" someone else asked.

One of the older elves spoke up, "We live."

"We must contact the council and tell them what has transpired," another elf suggested.

"Baw! Shit on 'em!" the elder spat. "We don't need those serpents ruling over us."

"We have always been free. Yndra was only here to aid us."

"Not this again," I sighed, shaking my head before navigating the crowd to leave while they continued to argue.

"The council will send a representative to look for her when she fails to attend their meetings. They will want to know why we didn't report the accident. It will not look good on us."

"That's exactly why they don't belong in Ashwood; they bring fear with them. We shouldn't be afraid of those who claim to help us."

"Going back to my question: What should we do?"

A strong elf sounded, "Now is the time to take a stand and not permit the scale heads entrance. Ashwood is home to the Dark Elves and no other!"

I heard Desynger's voice within the crowd suggest, "Saleth is right. We report the incident and request that a dragon guardian not be appointed to Ashwood."

"And if they refuse?"

"We defend our home."

As I walked up the steps to enter the cave out of Ashwood, I stopped a moment to look back at the city where I was born. I had been gone for so long, most people had forgotten about me, or perhaps they never cared. It's not like the Dark Elves are known for their hospitality.

Everyone was still gathered around the sunken obsidian tower, discussing their city's future, when I left Ashwood for the last time. I'm glad Pop sent me to live with the Light Elves. Although, I have fond memories of growing up in the darkness of Ashwood, my heart was in Lylandria with Jinxie. It took some time, but I grew accustomed to and quite fond of the sun. Perhaps in Magestice, I could find a cure to this vampirism I had been cursed with, so I may look upon the sun once again and feel its warmth upon my pale, cold skin.

CHAPTER XV

THE TEMPLE OF HIGH MAGIC

I reached the marble dragon archway leading into the elven city of Magestice. Two dragons were carved and placed on a moss-covered hill that bordered the road. They faced each other, their noses nearly touching. Directly ahead, there was a beautiful gazebo, and in the distance, over the cities many buildings, a tower reached into the sky.

Shaking my head that dragon statues had been erected and not elves, I said, "Well, come on, Horsem," and I led my undead centaur under the archway into the city.

Within the city, elflings played. They pointed wands that launched bolts of energy, but instead of causing harm, they left splats of color. Older elves planted and tended to flowers. The deeper into the city I walked, the more elves I saw sitting together discussing the intricacies of the arcane. They carried ancient grimoires and staves used to focus magical energy.

Houses and buildings were built two stories tall from wood on a base level of stone in a radial pattern around the central tower. Flowering vines grew up the walls and through sun-shaped balcony railings.

Horsem followed me through the magnificent city to the tower. We climbed the steps to the entrance where three bald elves with solid white eyes, wearing white robes, greeted us.

"Welcome to the Temple of High Magic," one of the elves greeted in a monotone voice.

"Thank you," I said to him, looking around for anyone else who may be watching.

One of the elves stepped forward and held his hands out to me, palms up. I looked down at them, curious what he wanted.

"This is known as the peaceful greeting, cousin," he explained. "Place your hands on mine to show you come without weapon or hostility."

"Of course."

I placed my open hands on his and instantly felt him probing my thoughts. I slapped his hands down, and the other two elves stepped forward to stand with him.

"I have come peacefully, but you are not welcome to probe my mind."

"Then you are not welcome to enter!" the elf told me with a stern voice. "Now, take your decrepit ass and get out of here."

"I know you're in there!" I yelled up at the tower. "I know you're watching through the eyes of your guards!"

The three elves flashed their hands at me. I felt a telekinetic force push against me, but instead of being moved by it, I pushed it back to them. Their bodies went hurling against the huge doors. The lead elf looked up at me, surprised he was outmatched.

"If that's what you want, I'll show you right here why I've come." I stripped the cover away that hid the obsidian chest on Horsem's back. "Within this chest is a dimensional prison containing the phoenix Arethil and the Dragon King Shadowrath. I recovered it from the dwarven kingdom. You must let me pass to place it under your care, High Elves of the temple," I urged, looking up at the marble tower, finding it odd that there were no windows.

The elves blocking my path stepped aside. "ADMITANCE GRANTED, ELF OF ASHWOOD," they said in unison with a thunderous voice just as the doors opened to a wall of white light.

"Come on, Horsem."

Through the brightly lit entrance, we stepped out from a stone archway to a small, moss-covered island encircled by a gently flowing stream. There were no temple walls, only a forest surrounded by mountains and waterfalls under a golden sky streaked with silver clouds. Trees and flowers soaked up the evening sun while elves studied and practiced various schools of magic.

"Well, I wasn't expecting this," I said in amazement of the Temple of High Magic's interior.

Horsem followed me across a stone bridge to explore this alternate world. I thought it strange to see elves sitting at tables reading among shelves of books, but perhaps, it never rained there.

We met two Wood Elves walking by us, heading for the magical doorway to leave. I was about to speak when their eyes turned to me, and my dark vision returned. The skin of everyone around me turned green and then to black before falling away, leaving their muscles and bones exposed. I closed my eyes and stood still, knowing the vision would pass soon.

"Welcome, cousin," I heard someone say to me. I cracked open one eye to make sure it was safe before opening both to see another Woodland Elf greeting me with a big smile. His long brown hair was braided and hung down his chest, reaching his leather belt. "Are you all right?"

Looking around, I saw that everyone appeared healthy, as they should. "Yes, for now."

"Which school of magic do you study?"

Noticing a green dragon brooch pinned to his collar, veiled by his long hair, my demeanor toward him changed. I gestured to the skeletal centaur standing behind me and answered, "Your powers of observation serve you well."

His smile quickly faded as he recognized his mistake.

"It was a good try," I nodded to ease the blow before walking by. "I'll show myself around, thank you."

Assuming the High Elves were teachers, I searched for a group learning advanced spellcasting.

An older elf approached. "Greetings." He looked over me and Horsem. "Are you here to join a class?"

"I'm here to speak with the High Elves," I answered as I watched an elf place her hands on the trunk of a willow tree and change the color of its leaves from green to white, making it appear as though the limbs were heavy with icicles.

Pointing up to the golden sky, the elf shook his head. "No one sees the High Elves. They created this dimension within the walls of the temple and now reside above us. When they are ready, they will choose those of us who they deem worthy to take their place," he explained, gesturing to all those around us.

Many students whispered to one another and laughed that I thought just anyone could see the High Elves. Their laughter came to an abrupt end when a beam of sunlight pierced the clouds to envelop me and my skeletal companion.

"Well, it looks like they're expecting me," I said to the astounded elves.

The light lifted us, and Horsem futilely tried to run. I broke into laughter at the sight of him running in air, but the elves below us cried that they deserved to be chosen.

Horsem and I were lifted just above the trees where I felt us pass through a magical barrier. The light that surrounded us went out, and I could feel a solid surface once again beneath my feet, but, it wasn't stone, it was transparent. Through the floor, I could see the elves below us wiping away their tears and watching the sky as the sun vanished in the west and immediately begin to rise in the east.

The room was too dark for me to see if there were walls, and it appeared empty except for three glass columns that emitted a soft glow. I looked up and saw a nude elf sitting atop each of the three columns. There was a Light Elf, Dark Elf, and a Woodland Elf. I couldn't tell whether they were male or female. Their eyes were closed in meditation. Their faces were etched with age, and their hair was extremely long, reaching to the floor. The Light Elf's hair was pale blue, the Dark Elf's was a soft black, and the Woodland Elf's was the color of fall leaves.

"My name is Ambros, son of Ambrosius of Ashwood. I have come to place this chest under your care. We must keep it hidden from the world. It was no longer safe where it was, so I brought it here."

The three elves said nothing. They were as still as the pillars they sat upon.

I unstrapped the obsidian chest from Horsem's back and placed it on the floor near the pillars. The three elves remained in silent meditation.

"I'll just show myself out, then," I announced before turning to look for an exit.

"You are powerful, Ambros, son of Ambrosius of Ashwood," the Woodland Elf said.

"You could one day take my place," the Dark Elf told me.

"And stay cooped up in the attic of this temple? I don't think so."

The Light Elf spoke up, saying, "The mind can create worlds limited only by its imagination."

Shaking my head, "You can't stay in here; we need your help ridding the world of dragons."

"The world is lost, Ambros," the Dark Elf spoke. "And we are too few to take it back. They may deny it, but deep down, all elves know the dragons will never relinquish control."

"So you'd rather dream of a better world 'til dragon or old age steals you from it?"

I saw them as skeletons sitting upon their glass columns, which wasn't a stretch from the way they already looked. I turned away, gritting my teeth.

"What do you see?" the Light Elf questioned.

"I see death," I answered, breathing deeply.

"Everyone dies, Ambros. We, too, will soon go to the Sun."

I looked back at them, seeing their skeletons fade into their sunken flesh.

The Light Elf then said, "You're welcome to study here at the temple."

"And we will watch over the chest," the Wood Elf announced, "but we cannot keep it safe forever."

"I understand. I just need time to figure things out."

"The Age of Elves is over. Except it."

"I won't. I can't," I argued. "I've seen too much to believe our race will be driven to extinction."

"Then we wish you luck on your quest, brother," the Dark Elf spoke before sending us back on a beam of light.

CHAPTER XVI

MEETING SYLVIA

For the next several years, I lived a quiet life in Magestice while studying at the Temple of High Magic. A bit large to keep indoors, I buried Horsem's remains outside my house and chose a smaller creature to assist me with my experiments. I resurrected a fairy that I named Stink. I let her drink my immortal blood from a small dish to see how it affected her. Her body healed to its former beauty, and her wings returned, allowing her to fly again, but her mind was still dull. She could only grunt and growl like the previous dead I had raised. After a week, her body began to decompose again until she lost her ability to fly. I tried submerging her in my blood for days like Byron had done to me only to get the same result.

While taking a break from trying to bring Stink back to life, I began studying what I called my necrovision. Instead of hiding my eyes to the dead visions, I opened my eyes to them. I discovered that my imagination triggered the visions and soon learned how to turn it on and off at will.

While looking out from my porch early one morning with my necrovision, I saw elves heading to the temple as animated cadavers. There was one, however, whose skin remained intact. Unlike everyone else who appeared dead, her skin was radiant.

"It cannot be!" I said to myself, making my way down the stairs with Stink flying closely behind me. I hurried to the temple and through the portal. Looking around, I didn't see her. "Curses!"

I reached for the arm of a nearby elf but withdrew it, not wanting to touch a stranger. "Did you see where she went?"

"Of whom do you speak?" I was asked politely.

The clarity of the question from one who appeared dead took me briefly by surprise. "The one with skin!" I described hastily.

The elf, still raw and bloody, tilted his head to the side. "Pardon?"

"She was just here, a Woodland Elf with brown hair," I described, but the elf shrugged his shoulders and shook his head. "Uh, books!" I remembered. "She carried an armful of books."

Pointing a raw finger through the trees to a group of book shelves, "Perhaps she returned her books to the library."

I thanked him and ran into the forest to an area with many tall book shelves filled with tomes and scrolls. There were a few elves studying that I saw with my necrovision, and, like a flower growing in a cemetery, I saw the beautiful elf maiden reading at a table. Her brown, luxurious tresses fell over her shoulders, and like most Woodland Elves, she had olive skin to help her blend into the forest.

Not wishing to interrupt, I walked over and sat quietly across from her. Stink hovered nearby. Taking another look around the library, I saw that everyone still appeared as rotting corpses, but the young woman across from me remained flawless. Closing my eyes for a moment, my vision returned to normal.

"You have nice skin," I finally spoke.

Without looking away from her book, she responded dryly, "Thanks. I was born with it."

I leaned forward to get a better view of the book she was reading. "Are you aware that you're reading that upside down?"

Again, she answered in the same neutral tone without turning her attention to me. "You're the one who's upside down. The book is right-side up to me."

"Hmm."

Overhead, Stink's wings were decaying to the point that she struggled to stay aloft. Her wings then began beating out of unison, causing her to fly in circles. When she could fly no more, she fell right down on the book that the pretty elf was reading. She screamed, slammed the book shut on the zombie fairy, and pushed herself back from the table.

"OH!" I flinched.

"Did you see it?" she asked. "It was hideous."

I smiled and explained softly, "Sometimes you have to be upside down to see the beauty in things."

A smile began to break across her face, and she slowly opened her book to find the fairy's broken corpse. "Oh, I didn't mean to kill it." She covered her nose and turned her face away. "Ew! The stink."

I stood up and reached over the table. I carefully scooped up the dead fairy into my hands. "I called her that, too," I admitted, examining the broken body, "but her name in life was Wink. She was cursed with a disease by a witch while freeing her kin from cages."

"My goodness."

With Stink's body draped over my left hand, I bit into the cheek of my right and squeezed a few drops of blood onto the fairy. Her flesh began to heal, so I placed her gently on the table and licked my wound closed.

After a moment, Stink was able to stand. It wasn't enough blood to heal her completely but enough for her to regain mobility. She stretched and twisted to align her broken limbs.

"I'm sorry I hurt you," the elf apologized to Stink but received no response.

I shook my head. "Don't expect forgiveness, for Stink is neither alive nor dead."

"She is undead," the elf said, surprising me that she knew. "I like the name Wink much better than Stink even though she does," she admitted with a cough.

The fairy's wings fluttered, and she rose from the table. Both, the elf maiden and I were happy to see Stink flying again.

"So you're learning necromancy to bring her back."

"To bring everyone back," I revealed.

She laughed. "That's quite a lofty goal. You may be here for a very long time."

"I could use an assistant, if you're interested," I

proposed to her with a charming smile.

"Your assistant!" she laughed. "I don't even know who you are."

"I'm me, and you are you," I answered, pointing at her and then to myself. "What else do you need to know?"

"But what is your name?" she pressed.

Playfully acting as though she should already know, I raised my hands to the sky and said, "By Arethil's beak!" I then bowed my head politely and introduced myself. "I am Ambros of Ashwood, born from Ambrosius, and once resident of the Light Elf city of Lylandria."

She returned the bow, answering modestly, "I am no one special, really, just Sylvia of Magestice."

"Oh, you are very special, more so than you know. What are you studying?" I asked to help her open up.

Examining the book she was reading, she saw that the pages were sticky with coagulated blood from where she had slammed it shut on Stink. "Well, I was studying Life Magic, but..."

"You're hired!" I blurted out.

"What if I decline?" she asked just as quickly.

"You have to," I pleaded. "I need your help." Looking at Stink flying aimlessly between the shelves of books, I said, "If not for me, do it for Stink. Do it for the zombie fairies."

With that, she broke into laughter. "Okay. Okay, you've convinced me. I'll be your assistant."

"Great! You won't regret it," I told her, standing from the table.

"And what will I be doing exactly?" she asked a

bit nervously. "Holding your cape?"

For a moment, I thought how great it would be to wear one before answering, "I don't have a cape, but if you'll hold it for me, perhaps I should make one."

Sylvia closed her book and stood from her chair, saying, "Then perhaps we should get started."

"YES!" I exclaimed, clenching my fists in excitement. Snapping my fingers, a green cape instantly formed around my neck and rolled down to my feet. I turned away from Sylvia and kicked back, causing the cape to float out from me as I began to walk out of the library.

Sylvia giggled. "This should be interesting."

We began by getting to know each other. We left the bustling temple to take an evening stroll through the city. We talked about our childhood, our family, and our friends. I knew she suspected I was undead, but I didn't reveal to her that I was a vampire right away. For the next several months, we studied, tested, and worked. She wasn't all that gifted in magic, but I knew I needed her.

CHAPTER XVII

THE ALLURE OF THE SUN

It was late. Dawn would be coming soon. I paced the floor of my candlelit dwelling, trying to wrap my mind around the problem I knew must have a solution. I could hear music and laughter from outside where a festival was taking place.

Magestice was an eventful city. Day and night, something was always happening, whether it was dinner parties, magic shows, or games. Sylvia told me that a small number of Woodland Elves grew tired of the busy city. They wanted a quieter life like the one described to them by Light Elves who had traveled there from Lylandria. Early one morning, they packed their bags and set out to build a new town to call home. They settled in a beautiful area to the south that they named Sungrove.

As often as possible, Sylvia traveled to Sungrove to visit her best friend, Delwen, who had married and left with the group who settled there. I went with her a few times before growing bored of the trip. That's where she was this particular night. She had been gone a week already, and I didn't expect her back for another week.

My research had consumed me. I often went for days without feeding. I felt I was so close to discovering the secret, I could smell it. Because I have difficulty remembering when events take place, Sylvia helped me transcribe and organize my memories along a timeline that she painted on my walls. She used pins and varying lengths of twine to connect notes to points along the timeline. There were so many notes that we ran out of room on the walls, so we had to pin pages to the ceiling. The floor, although free of paper, was covered in arcane symbols written in blood that had long since dried.

"To truly bring someone back from the dead, I must reconnect their thoughts and memories to their body," I repeated over and over to myself as I glanced over my countless notes while my mind worked toward a solution. "I can create a body, but their thoughts... Their thoughts..." I spotted a name written on a scrap of parchment that I had tacked to the wall. "Stenwick," I read aloud. "Stenwick attempted to travel back in time to convince the elves from dividing during the Great Winter. He knew he couldn't change the timeline, but perhaps he could create a new one from any point in history. Time isn't just a measurement between events; it is a dimension that retains everything! Like my memories, they just need to be collected and reorganized on a new timeline!"

I suddenly felt overwhelmed by the revelation.

Combing my fingers through my hair, I began laughing that I finally discovered the missing piece of the puzzle. "Why did it take me so long? It seems so simple, now. I need some air."

I stepped out onto the balcony and took a deep breath of the cool night air. The room that I lived in was on the second floor of one of the student homes. I could see many elves walking the dimly-lit streets. Groups played music while others dined together. There were some who shot lightning into the sky where it would then jump from cloud to cloud high above the city.

Now that much of the stress had lifted, my stomach growled to remind me it had been empty for too long. I walked back into the house, out the door, and down the steps to venture into the forest for a late night snack. With so many magic users in this city, I wouldn't dare attempt to feed on someone.

"They would burn me at the stake!" I chuckled to myself. "I'm sure I would make a delicious kabob, though."

I made my way through the busy streets to the edge of the city where I ran up a grassy hill into the forest. I had a path worn from where I'd gone out to set traps in a small clearing. The magic I had cast to trap a rabbit had already faded before catching anything. Checking the hole I had dug, I could see that the vegetables I baited the trap with was gone.

"I need something more filling than a rabbit tonight, anyway," I said while rubbing my aching tummy.

Movement in the forest caught my attention. Between the trees, I could see a small deer with his eyes locked onto me. My heart rate quickened, and I felt my fangs lengthen with the anticipation of piercing its flesh and draining it dry. The deer darted through the forest to escape me. My sandals found traction in the packed soil, and I sped after it. Using a bit of elvish magic, I made a noise that got the young deer's attention. It stood still in a moonlit clearing. When I reached the clearing, I immediately felt it.

"Son of a witch!" I cursed myself.

Looking at the ground, I saw that I was standing in a circle of small stones. The deer vanished; it was an elaborate illusion. I shook my head and laughed at my predicament. I began to hear someone applauding, but it sounded muffled. I then saw Byron rise out of the earth like a shadow taking shape and his clapping became clear.

"Bravo, my boy! Bravo!" he congratulated. "You've fallen victim to your own trap. It's quite a clever spell, I must say."

I punched the invisible barrier that surrounded me, causing a vibration that made it visible for a moment.

"Once something steps into the circle, they cannot escape until the entrapment spell wears off," he continued, walking around the circle of stones. Holding up a finger, he added, "But the real genius of this spell is that it cuts you off from using magic during the spell's duration. It's an entrapment layered with dispel."

Lightning crackled from his fingers, striking the barrier without penetrating it.

I pointed at the stones encircling me. "What's with all this? You mean to tell me, you had to enchant all these tiny stones to use for this entrapment spell?" I shook my head in disappointment. "You are no more than an amateur magician who I wouldn't pay to entertain children," I said to anger him.

Byron stepped right up to the edge of my magical prison so that we were face to face. With him wearing Pop's body, it was like I was looking at my future self, and, in a way, I was.

"I am going to cast away this fragile shell and possess your immortal body. Your knowledge and power will be mine to command, but you, Ambros, you will be extinguished forever."

Motioning toward the space within the ring of stones, I said, "Come on in, buddy. There's plenty of room in here for the two of us."

"No, thank you," he smiled. "I think I'll wait a few more minutes before I remove the spell."

Through the trees, I could see the darkness fading as dawn approached. A big smile spread across my face while popping my neck and fingers. "Well, I don't have all night. How about we hurry this along?" I announced before digging a thumbnail into my palm. "You don't have much time if you're going to step into this body; it doesn't like sunlight, you know."

I then wiped the thick blood that oozed from the wound onto the wall of my prison. As the blood ran down, it caused the spell to weaken, melting a hole.

Our eyes were locked, waiting for the moment to strike. Byron's fingers twitched with anticipation. Right when the stream of blood reached the ring of stones, the entrapment spell collapsed and Byron threw his hands out, launching black, ethereal chains to hold me. They wrapped around my left arm and right leg. I summoned a dagger with my bleeding hand, but I didn't attack Byron. I spun the dagger around and plunged it into my own heart!

"HAGH! HAGH!" Byron expelled a harsh laugh. "You're making it too easy for me. Your blood will heal your wounds."

I, too, began to laugh as my blood was pulled into the ethereal realm through the dagger piercing my heart. "It is the blood that I'm destroying."

As my flesh began to shrivel, Byron realized what was happening. "NO, YOU FOOL!" he yelled, retracting the chains that bound me. "What are you doing?"

I struggled to look upon the sun as first light broke through the trees. "I can hear it," I announced. My legs became too weak to hold me up, so I eased myself to the ground. "The sun calls me home."

Without blood to slow its effects, rays of the sun burned away my flesh, leaving my bones to crumble to dust, yet, I watched it all unfold.

"So that's what death feels like. Let's do it again." My voice resonated strangely to me. I extended my hands and saw that they were made of fire.

Byron watched as I rose above him, his face reflecting feelings of amazement and panic. "You found them! He will soon call upon me to command his armies. The world is doomed!"

I took a deep breath, feeling my body grow hot. I exhaled, lowering my temperature to a level where I could take a more familiar form. I turned to the morning sun. I could feel its light permeate my skin. It felt like a warm fire on a cold night, calling me to come closer. Still floating a few feet above the ground, I turned away from the sun to find Byron kneeling before me.

"I accept defeat," he announced with his head

bowed. "Your power has grown far beyond my own, Ambros of Ashwood. I would serve you, were I not bound to my master."

"Your master, Shadowrath, has not been freed," I revealed to him. "Both he and Arethil are still confined to their dimensional prison. I was able to speak to Arethil briefly. She granted me a portion of her immense power so that I may continue the work she began eons ago."

"The world has changed much since the elder days. You will have to destroy everything before attempting to rebuild it," Byron advised.

Turning back to the sun, I told him, "I need time to think how best to use this power."

"What would you have me do?"

Smiling, I answered, "Hope your master never escapes."

I flew through the forest at an unimaginable speed toward the morning sun. Tree limbs passed harmlessly through me. Leaving the forest behind, I sped through the atmosphere into space.

I thought of Sylvia. She was still in Sungrove visiting her friends, Delwen and her husband. I stopped a moment to look back at the Earth. The view was stunning. The planet was a spinning, blue sphere with patches of white clouds encircling it. On the surface, I could see a tiny spark of light. I focused my eyes on the light, and with my knowledge of magic and newly gifted powers, I was able to see all the way to Delwen's house and through its walls to see Sylvia sitting at a table talking to Delwen as she prepared breakfast. The light that I saw came from within Sylvia. I had passed onto her the same fire that Arethil passed to me. Feeling confident she will be fine, I continued my journey to the Sun.

It took only moments to traverse the great distance to the fiery orb. I walked across its turbulent surface. Its blazing heat felt wonderful, so I plunged into its liquid depths.

ACT III

2011 AD

CHAPTER XVIII

THE SON BECOMES THE FATHER

"I understand, now, what Pop meant when he told me that I must recover his spirit from the blood," Ambros said to Manius after finishing his tale.

Everyone looked at Manius and then back to Ambros, unsure what was about to happen.

Manius' lips tightened and tears welled up in his eyes before finally speaking. "Ambros, I am sorry for everything I have done." He brought his hands up to cover his mouth and he began sobbing. "I brought about the extinction of entire races and destroyed their history. I did . . . what I believed . . . was right."

Ambros stepped closer to hug him, and Manius collapsed into his arms, crying. "It's all right," Ambros consoled him. "It's all right. You've done nothing to warrant an apology. You did what you had to do; what you were meant to do; what my father could not do. You completed the journey that Pop set you on millennia ago."

"Are you going to take away my power?"

"I am going to take away your pain," Ambros answered.

He pulled Manius' head to the side, exposing his neck. "How 'bout we do this the old fashioned way?"

Manius didn't struggle, nor did he try to escape. He accepted his fate. Ambros opened his mouth and fangs extended before biting into his throat. We all waited quietly as the Dark Elf drank from him. I turned away, unable to watch. Seraphine took hold of my hand but said nothing.

Ambros drained him to the point of death before gently passing his body to Vistilia. She eased him to the floor where she rested his head on her leg. She ran her fingers through his hair and looked at him lovingly.

Manius' eyes cracked open enough to focus on her. "I love you."

"I know you do," she smiled. "I love you, too."

Ambros seemed to be meditating, standing perfectly still. "I can see them," he whispered. "I can see them." His eyes opened and a look of complete understanding washed over him. "Pop . . . I mean, I am a genius."

With a beaming smile, he told Sylvia, "We have work to do, my dear." He raised a finger and said to the rest of us, "Don't go anywhere."

Sylvia rushed over and threw her arms around him. A sphere of bright light formed around them, and they vanished.

"Where are they off to in such a hurry?" I wondered.

Manius' eyes closed, and he stopped breathing. Vistilia leaned over and kissed him. When she pulled away, I saw a hint of smoke rise from his mouth. His lips turned black, and a spark of fire began burning away his flesh. His chest burst into flames, but Vistilia didn't push away his body. She wasn't harmed by the fire. His flesh burned away, revealing a body of golden light within. His bones crumbled to dust across Vistilia's lap, and the golden light appeared to solidify, taking Manius' form. Opening his eyes, he breathed deeply. A flash of fire lit his pupils before returning to normal.

Vistilia welcomed him back with a kiss and allowed him to stand. "How do you feel?"

"Perfect," he answered humbly. Looking around, "Where's Ambros?"

Teleporting into the room, a young Dark Elf announced, "I'm back!" He wore white clothing, accented with red and gold.

"And Sylvia?" Manius finished his question, looking at the boy. A big smile spread across his face, and he hugged the elf. "Look at you! You're young again."

"I prefer being a kid. And Sylvia, well, she's tending to the garden," the boy answered with a suspicious grin.

"What garden? Where have you been?" Manius questioned.

"How 'bout we escape this icy dungeon and go somewhere nicer?" he asked before surrounding us all in a bright light.

Even though I could not yet see where we were whisked off to, I knew we were no longer in the arctic facility; I could hear birds singing, and a warm breeze brought the sweet smell of honeysuckle. The light faded, and my eyes adjusted to see a stunning landscape of fruit trees, fresh flowers, and large mushrooms.

I then realized I was standing in the sunshine, unharmed by its light, and I remembered that Dirk had siphoned away my power. I had only been a vampire for a few short years, but that was still enough time to forget how wonderful the sun felt on my skin. I breathed in the sweet air and exhaled my stress away.

"Wow! It's beautiful," Seraphine whispered.

We all realized how overdressed we were for this warm climate, so we began removing layers of clothing and leaving them on the grass.

Looking around, Manius asked, "Where is this place?"

"The colors seem too vibrant to be real," I stated, touching the soft petals of a daisy before picking it for Seraphine.

She smiled and put the flower in her hair.

Vistilia put a hand on Ambros' shoulder. "You've created quite a paradise. I'm proud of you."

"Created? What do you mean, created? Where are we?" Manius asked her.

"Oh, this is my own planet, an alternate version of Earth," the young Ambros answered.

"Wait," Manius stopped him. "You created your own planet?"

"Well, I had to for the other inhabitants," he answered. "I retrieved the souls of my kin from the oceans of time, giving them life again, and used my knowledge of death to eradicate it."

As if on cue, we heard laughter and turned to see elves playfully chasing one another among a nearby crop of fruit trees. Like Ambros, they were barely teenagers. A boy and girl in particular caught my attention. They were twins with strawberry blond hair.

"Kieran," I called. "Kelena."

They stopped, curious who called them and ran over. They looked at me as though they had difficulty remembering.

"Kevin?" Kieran finally asked in disbelief.

"It is Kevin!" his sister cried, and they both hugged me.

"You've only been gone a few hours, and you've already forgotten me," I joked.

"Hours? No, we awoke here with the others nearly two centuries ago," Kieran recalled.

"Funny thing about time," Ambros spoke up with a joyful tear in his eye. "Not only does it flow differently depending on where you are, but everything is recorded within it. The trick is locating the exact moment in time where each and every elf died, and then plucking their consciousness from their mind."

"Why did Ambrosius transfer his consciousness to me, leaving you to wander the earth alone?" Manius asked him.

"We're actually the same person, he and I," the boy sounded strangely adult, "but if you think of us as separate entities, the son's purpose was to learn to reach beyond the physical to manipulate the unseen with power acquired from the phoenix Arethil. The father, on the other hand, needed time unburdened by life's everyday struggles to study and understand time itself. He needed to understand not just why he existed but why everything exists."

"And why does all this exist?" Vistilia asked

with a big smile on her face, clearly already knowing the answer.

"What's a house without inhabitants?" I answered the question with a question. "You said it yourself, Vistilia, our universe is a simulation running on a computer in your universe." Remembering Ambros' story, I added, "And like the elves of Lylandria were discussing: We are part of the universe. While we study it, the universe is studying itself."

"We are what make the universe alive," Seraphine said enthusiastically.

"Now life from Earth has spread to a parallel universe," Ambros explained. "And once more, the elves can live peacefully in paradise."

Vistilia plucked a flower to smell. "But, eventually, your people will become bored with paradise," she remarked before crushing the flower in her hand and wiping it away. "They will want more from life. They will crave knowledge, seek adventure, and test the very fabric of this universe you've created for them until they push through it just as you did mine." A smile broke across her face. "One day, you'll understand what I mean, and you will give them what they long for. You'll release destruction and despair upon your world."

"Dirk," I heard Kieran voice fearfully under his breath.

Grief struck Ambros as he looked over the beautiful world he had created.

"Dirkonus is but a shadow of a man," Manius stated, "eroded by time itself. If he should ever escape his dark prison, he would surely unleash his wrath upon you and your world."

"And your people will lose their paradise," Vistilia added grimly. "They will feel pain; they will lose hope; they will know death; and they will ascend," she proclaimed.

"The cycle starts anew," Ambros whispered, imagining the journey ahead.

Seraphine suggested, "Then you should enjoy it while it lasts."

Ambros smiled and took a deep breath. "You're right. I shouldn't let an uncertain future dishearten me."

"Where is Sylvia?" I asked. "Can't she help?"

Ambros pointed up to the cerulean sky. "She left to create her own world. I couldn't leave; this is the home I've wanted my entire life."

Looking at Kieran and Kelena, I couldn't help but smile. Although they had been there for centuries, they appeared wide-eyed and youthful. Their sun kissed skin and strawberry blond hair was radiant.

"What is it?" Kelena asked.

"Why are you staring at us?" Kieran chuckled.

"Nothing," I answered quickly before adding, "You're younger, now, than you were when I knew you."

With a quizzical look, Kieran questioned, "When you knew us?"

"You still know us," his sister corrected me, laughing.

A third elf came to stand with us. She had long, dark hair tied up in pigtails and wore a black dress.

"And what's your name?" I asked the girl.

Slipping her hand in Kieran's, she answered sweetly, "Tess."

A big smile lit my face. I was so happy for

Kieran; he had his childhood sweetheart back, and she was no longer the 8" tall fairy she was in her previous life. She was now a Woodland Elf, the same as Kieran.

Elves of all types came running to see who had visited their splendid world. Their soft steps were as quiet as the wind. They, too, appeared young, but I knew otherwise. I knew they retained memories of their life on Earth. Dozens encircled us and sat in the grass. Countless others stood back and observed from afar.

"Besides Stenwick, we're all here," Ambros announced while we looked over everyone.

Seraphine met the eyes of a young Light Elf girl sitting among the crowd with rose-colored hair.

"Including your parents," Ambros said to her.

Seraphine and the girl covered their mouth in unison. The girl took hold of a blond-haired boy next to her. They stood and made their way through the multitude of elves to reach us. Seraphine left my side to meet them with tears and open arms. She had told me that she had no memory of her parents, but she must have seen something in the girl that triggered a feeling. Perhaps she saw herself.

I could see they were talking, but without the supernatural hearing that I lost when Dirk took my power, I could not hear what was being said between them. Seraphine looked back at me, briefly, and wiped tears from her eyes.

"What do you think she will do?" Vistilia whispered.

The question worried me. What was she going to do?

"Her parents are here. Her people are here," Vistilia reminded me. Pointing at the picturesque vista around us, she asked, "Would you leave paradise? Could you?"

I shook my head but wondered what Seraphine would choose. How would my life change without her? Seraphine's interest in the future of technology and love for jogs at the park has rubbed off on me. I have even adopted her morning and evening yoga routine. I like the person I've become since she's been in my life. And I know her life has changed since we've been together. She has become quite a gamer geek. She's played everything from Zelda and Castlevania to Halo and The Elder Scrolls. I've also broadened her taste in music, introducing her to hard rock and heavy metal. She has also grown fond of video game and movie soundtracks.

Behind me, elves were speaking with Manius. With fiery tears streaming down his face, he was on his knees apologizing for destroying the elves' last great city, Magestice. Accepting his heartfelt apology, they each hugged him.

I covered my mouth and yawned. Checking my watch to see what time it was, I shook my head at my foolishness. My watch displayed the time for where I lived, not where I was. I then looked up to try determining the time from the position of the sun. It appeared to be midday.

Seeing what I had done, Ambros stepped over to speak to me. "It's always midday here."

"What about the other side of this planet?" I asked curiously.

"You may want to sit in the shade, so your head doesn't get burned," he suggested, pointing to my shaved head. He then motioned for me to follow him. The surrounding elves divided to allow us passage.

We walked to an apple tree where he reached up and picked two. Holding one of the apples still, he moved the other slowly around it. "The planet isn't perfectly round. There's a bulge that is held by the sun's gravitational pull. As we orbit the sun, we are kept in direct alignment with it, and the other side remains in darkness."

He bit one of the apples and tossed me the other. I followed him to a group of large, purple and white mushrooms that grew just over head high in the perpetual shade of the forest. We sat beneath them and ate our apples while watching the others.

Between bites, I asked, "So now that you've created this perfect world, what will you do?"

"I think I may remove my power to live as a normal elf."

His answer surprised me. "What? How will you do that?"

"The power I was given by Arethil resides in my blood. To expel it, I must bleed it out. I know it sounds dangerous, but I know I will survive."

"But why would you give up all that power?" I asked him. "There's so much more you can do."

Taking the last bite of apple, he extended his hand holding the core. It left his grasp, flying away from us to rest on a patch of mossy earth. The apple core shriveled and rotted away within seconds. A tiny sprout protruded from the decayed matter, reaching to the sun. The sprout grew leaves and limbs. It grew taller and stronger until it bore fruit. All this happened within mere moments of the apple core hitting the ground. A freshly ripened apple pulled free of the tree and flew to Ambros' waiting hand. Taking a bite, he seemed bored at how easy it was.

"I no longer need all this power," he answered.
"I accomplished all that I set out to do."

"So you were able to bring Jinxie back from the ashes?"

Smiling, he pointed to an elf girl standing beneath a tree with other elves. Her hair was the color of dreamsicle cheesecake. As if sensing his gaze, she kissed her fingers and waved at him.

"I want to live a simple life," he professed, still looking at her. "I wouldn't feel the need to change things if they were outside my power. I could just live."

I finished my apple and tossed the core, but it didn't rot away like the other.

"Would you like another?" Ambros asked.

"No, thank you," I answered softly, leaning back against the trunk of the mushroom. I breathed in deeply the warm breeze and closed my eyes. "This place is wonderful," I whispered before drifting off to sleep.

EPILOGUE

My eyes opened to see my bedroom ceiling. I slowly pulled my left arm free from the covers to check my watch. It was 8:06, Sunday morning.

"Ugh, it's morning," I grumbled. I closed my eyes for a moment and caught flickering visions of another world. I saw a picturesque landscape inhabited by elves. Large, puffy clouds drifted across a bright, midday sky. I breathed in deeply the sweet fragrance of flowers carried on a summer breeze. Exhaling, I opened my eyes again to find myself in my room.

"It couldn't have been a dream, could it?" I asked myself.

I pulled back the covers to get out of bed and opened the blinds to let the morning sun brighten my room. I stood next to the bed and began my yoga routine. Clearing my mind, I focused on breathing while

I stretched my muscles. I felt constricted by my own skin. The strength I once felt was gone. I got down on the floor and began doing pushups. As a vampire, I could do countless pushups, but now, I could feel myself getting tired with each push. My arms shook. My eyes watered. I cursed myself for being weak. I pushed until I could push no more, collapsing to the floor. I was exhausted. It took a moment to control my breathing before rolling over on my back and wiping the tears from my face.

Dirk stood over me, shaking a glowing fist in my face. "You'll never be good enough!"

"NO!" I screamed and scrambled to get up, finding no one there. I rushed to the nightstand where I grabbed my knife. I took a quick glance under the bed, the closet, and down the hall. I searched over the entire house, knife at the ready, wearing nothing but underwear, finding no one.

"What am I doing?" I laughed at myself, sheathing the foot long tanto. "This wouldn't have hurt him."

Convinced that my imagination conjured the vision of Dirk, I went back to my bedroom. I slipped on a pair of shorts and a white tee shirt before going to the kitchen.

"I don't need blood anymore, so what do I want to drink, now?"

I looked outside to see the sun shining brightly. I opened the door and walked out onto the carport. I stepped to the edge, where the shade met the light. I took a breath and another step forward to stand in the morning sun. Like on Ambros' beautiful world, the sun didn't harm me. I looked up at the clear sky and closed my eyes to allow the warm sun to penetrate my eyelids. "Tea," I whispered to myself. "I haven't had tea in a long time."

After another moment in the sun, I went back indoors and searched the kitchen cabinets for Seraphine's spiced tea that she called Aralas. After finding it sealed in a small tin, I began heating water in her electric kettle. I measured out a tablespoon of the loose leaf tea into an infuser before placing it into a big, glass mug. While waiting by the kettle, listening to the steaming water, I thought about my life.

I was 34 years old and no longer immortal. If I live to be as old as my grandpa, then I had already reached midlife. And what had I accomplished? I had never married. I had no kids. My books rarely sell among the ever-deepening sea of literary works being published each year. I suffer from avoidant personality disorder, so it's astounding I even released my fantastic tales for the whole world to read and criticize.

My water had begun to boil, so I poured it over the tea leaves and placed the lid on the infuser to hold the heat in while it steeped. After starting the timer on my watch, I stood at the window and looked out.

"What do I want to do today? Perhaps I'll go for a run at the park," I answered myself.

When the tea had steeped long enough, I removed the infuser from the mug and added a splash of almond milk. I raised the mug to my nose and breathed deeply the aromatic steam before taking a sip. The black tea's complexity of hazelnut and cinnamon with almond milk was delightful.

Just as I was about to take another sip, I heard a car pull into the driveway. I listened for who it may be, but I no longer had supernatural hearing. I no longer had enhanced senses. I was a normal person in a normal world.

I carefully sat the full mug on the counter and walked to the door. I opened it just as she started to insert a key to unlock it.

"Kevin," she said, throwing her arms around me. "Good morning, sweetie."

I hugged her tightly. "Seraphine, you're here," I said, surprised.

"Aww, Kevin. Of course, I'm here. Where else would I be?"

"I thought you would have stayed in Ambros' paradise."

She smiled. "I belong here with you," she professed sweetly, taking my hand in hers. "And besides, they don't have internet," she added, and we both laughed.

She picked up two bags of groceries that she had sat on a little outside table and came inside.

She breathed in the smell of my freshly brewed tea. "What do you think?" she asked while putting the groceries away.

"It's great! Would you like a cup?"

"Please."

"You go ahead and take this one. I'll brew another cup for me."

Just as she raised the mug to her lips, I added, "I only took a sip, so I didn't infect it with too many of my cooties."

She began giggling and had to sit the mug down so she wouldn't spill it.

I refilled the water kettle and added a bit more

tea leaves to the infuser.

She walked over to me and said, "Circle," and kissed me on the nose. She said, "Circle," again and kissed me on the lips. Wrapping her arms around me, she squeezed me twice, saying "Square. Square. Now, you have it everywhere."

Acting as if I were crying, I wailed, "No! No!" and we both laughed.

I poured the steaming water over the leaves and allowed it to steep.

Noticeably trying to contain her excitement, she said, "I received a phone call this morning."

"Yeah? Who was it?"

"I got a job!"

"Well, congratulations! That's great!" I hugged her. "What exactly will you be doing?"

"It's a government funded project," she began with a look that it was a big deal. "I will be designing segments of DNA to be added to the human genome."

"Oh, wow! That sounds exciting."

I finished preparing my tea, so we sat at the dining room table together. Noticing a black skull pendant that she wore on a leather necklace, I pointed to it. "Where did you get that?"

She reached up and rubbed the pendant between her thumb and forefinger. "Ambros gave me this. It serves as a link to his world in case I decide to go," she answered, reading the emotion in my face.

My lips twisted in a failed attempt to hide my sorrow, and I took a deep breath. "Perhaps we can vacation there after you settle into your new job," I suggested to cover my fear of her leaving me to return to her people.

"That would be the perfect vacation spot," she responded. "In the meantime, I'd like to get some equipment to use here where I could study DNA."

"Human DNA?"

"Werewolf," she reluctantly clarified.

"Werewolf!" I repeated, remembering when I was trapped inside Kieran's underground sanctuary with his bloodthirsty sister mere inches away from devouring me alive.

"I'm curious if there are any clues within my genetic code to how we originated, and what makes us immortal."

"How do you plan on getting a blood sample?" I asked before realizing what she had just said. "Wait! Your genetic code?"

She took a swallow of tea, noticeably hesitant to answer my question. "Well, do you remember when I went into hiding after being attacked by werewolves?"

I covered my mouth in shock at what she was implying, and she nodded her head, answering the question that I could not ask.

"So, what's it like?" I finally asked.

A slow laugh began churning up from within her. "Well, I'm no longer a vegetarian."

My eyes widened, and, for a moment, I didn't know whether to laugh or run.

She took my hand to comfort me. "Don't be afraid."

THE END

OR ONLY THE BEGINNING?

www.ingramcontent.com/pod-product-compliance
Lightning Source LLC
Chambersburg PA
CBHW070855250626
47159CB00003B/1077